A FIGHT TO THE DEATH

It was only by the grace of God and his wilderness-honed reflexes that Zach kept the Grim Reaper at bay. Backing against a table, he shoved it out of his way. Only he shoved too hard and the table upended instead, and in doing so, its legs became entangled with his. He tried to stay upright but couldn't.

In a bound the Goliath reached him. Zach's arms were seized and he was whipped violently about, first in one direction, then another. Zach aimed a kick that connected with the other's knee. A hiss escaped the giant's lips. He pushed with all his might.

Zach braced for impact with the wall. But he struck something softer. The curtains, as it turned out, which were not enough to slow him down and stop him from striking the window itself. He clutched for the jamb, but then cool air was on his face and he dropped like a rock toward the ground three stories below.

The *Wilderness* series:

#43
WILDERNESS
VENGEANCE

David Thompson

LEISURE BOOKS NEW YORK CITY

Dedicated to Judy, Joshua, and Shane.
And that Sunflower Bigfoot, Larry.

A LEISURE BOOK®

August 2004

Published by

Dorchester Publishing Co., Inc.
200 Madison Avenue
New York, NY 10016

ISBN 0-8439-5255-5

Printed in the United States of America.

Visit us on the web at www.dorchesterpub.com.

#43
WILDERNESS
VENGEANCE

AUTHOR'S NOTE

The entries in the King journal detailing Evelyn's abduction and the subsequent search comprise over fifty pages. This book covers only the first five.

Chapter One

The man came down the narrow street slowly. He paused often to look behind him and listen. At that late hour his were the only footsteps, the sigh of the wind the only other sound.

On his right a house reared out of the darkness. None of the windows was lit. The yard had suffered neglect and the weathervane on the roof creaked. The gate creaked, too, when the man opened it and moved along an overgrown path to the porch. He climbed cautiously. A brass knocker hung on the door, but he used his knuckles instead, rapping lightly so as not to wake any of the neighbors.

When there was no response, the man knocked again. While he waited he shifted his weight from one foot to the other and clenched and unclenched his hands. At last there was the scrape of metal on metal, and the door swung in on raspy hinges.

A black cavity yawned before him.

The man started to take a step but hesitated. "Hello?" he said softly. "Is anyone there?"

From the depths of the house came a muffled noise the man could not identify. He repeated his question and when there was no reply he turned to go.

"Do you have the note you were sent?"

The man gave a start and nearly tripped over his feet. "Yes," he said, probing the inky interior. He fished the note from a pocket and held it out. "See? I have it right here."

A hand twice the size of his took it and withdrew into the dark. "So you are Mr. Benjamin, is that correct?"

"Yes, I'm Ira Benjamin. But how can you read that when there's no light?"

"Please follow me. The others have already arrived, and it would not do to keep the mistress waiting."

"Mistress?" Benjamin repeated. "That's a strange way to refer to her. Who are you? Her butler?"

"This way, if you please." The voice came from farther in.

Benjamin stepped over the threshold and immediately couldn't see his hand when he held it in front of his face. "Can't you light a lamp? What's to keep me from walking into a wall?"

"Follow the sound of my voice. Keep walking

and in a few moments we will be at the cellar. That's where the others are."

"Who are these others you keep talking about?" Benjamin strained to hear the man's footsteps, but he moved as silently as a cat.

"You will know them when you see them. All will be made clear," was the enigmatic answer. "Keep following my voice. That's it. A little more. Another few yards, and here we are."

A door opened and a rectangle of pale light spilled into the hallway. For the first time Benjamin saw the other man clearly, and he involuntarily shivered. "My goodness! You're a big one."

Over seven feet tall if he was an inch, Benjamin's guide wore a short black jacket and black pants, the jacket sculpted to his muscular frame like a second skin. "I'll take that as a compliment, sir. After you, if you please."

A flight of stairs led down. Benjamin descended partway, then stopped. Below was a musty basement, the walls cracked and pitted, the overhead beams caked with grime. "Why in the world are we meeting in this godforsaken place?"

"Because I deemed it prudent," said a melodious female voice with a hard undercurrent. "Please, won't you join us?"

Benjamin continued to the bottom. A table had been placed near the left-hand wall. Behind it sat a woman all in black with a stylish hat and a lacy veil that covered half her face. "You're the one," he said.

"Yes," the woman confirmed. "You will soon be

a thousand dollars richer, thanks to me." She gestured. "Be seated."

Five chairs had been set up facing the table. Four were occupied by men Benjamin recognized. To say he was shocked did not do him justice. "It can't be! Do you mean to say I wasn't the only one?"

"I do not believe in leaving anything to chance," the woman said. "Which is why I'm wearing this veil. Should any of you have an ill-advised change of heart, you won't be able to report me to the authorities."

In the first chair sat a man of sixty or more, his hair nearly white, his face a latticework of wrinkles. His name was Webber and until recently he had made his living as a carpenter. "You too, Benjamin?" he said. "I never suspected how many were involved."

"Here I reckoned I was the only one," said the second man, Hurst, who in his time had eaten more than a few too many pies and sweet cakes.

"So did I," said the next one. Theodore Beckman was young and pale and had spectacles perched on the end of his thin nose.

"Let's make it unanimous," declared the fourth, a middle-aged fellow whose clothes were better than the other men's but not as expensively made as the woman's or her manservant's. Phillip Monroe owned a thriving mercantile.

Making himself comfortable in the last chair, Benjamin said to the woman, "You're taking an awful risk. If the authorities ever find out, they'll throw you behind bars, female or not."

Her vehemence was as unexpected as it was unsettling. She smacked the table and growled with animal-like intensity, "I would take the same risk a thousand times over to see him pay for what he did."

"I take it you are not fond of the gentleman?" Phillip Monroe asked.

"Fond?" She hissed like a lynx about to strike. "He is scum! A half-breed pig who deserves to suffer without end for the lives he has taken."

Benjamin waited for her to regain her composure, then posed the question, "If you hate him so much, Miss Borke, why did you go to so much trouble to have him found innocent?"

The woman stiffened, and for more than a minute she was still. Then she slowly raised her veil, revealing an exquisitely lovely oval face with piercing green eyes and full red lips. "So you have figured out who I am? Then there is no further need for subterfuge."

"It wasn't hard," Benjamin said. "There was talk at the trial about a sister. But she never showed. Then each of us were slipped these notes." He placed his on the table. "Two plus two usually equals four."

"Quite perceptive of you," the woman complimented him, then proudly confirmed, "Yes, I am Athena Borke."

Hurst was looking at her in confusion. "I don't get this. You're the sister? And you want the breed dead? Then why in God's name did you tamper with the jury?"

"Exactly," Theodore Beckman said. "Had it not

been for you, we would have found him guilty. His neck would have been stretched on the gallows by now."

Athena removed her hat and placed it beside her. "I suppose it won't hurt to satisfy your curiosity. After all, you five have done me an inestimable service. I am forever in your debt."

"The thousand dollars you promised will make us even," Hurst said, and laughed far louder than his comment called for.

A thin smile curled Athena's fine mouth. "Artemis and Phineas Borke were my older brothers. I might note that I loved them as fully and dearly as any sister has ever loved her brothers since the dawn of time."

Hurst laughed again. "My sisters hate me. We always fought like cats and dogs when we were young."

Athena ignored the comment. "When I learned that my brothers had been murdered by the half-breed, I came straightaway to see that their deaths were properly avenged."

Phillip Monroe said skeptically, "By having him set free? I'm afraid I agree with the others. Your logic eludes me. Why not let the court deal with him? Let the punishment fit the crime?"

"Hanging is hardly fitting," Athena said with intense bitterness. "They would slip a rope around his neck and throw a lever, and in thirty seconds it would be over. There's little pain, little suffering. And I want the breed to suffer as I have suffered. To hurt as I have hurt."

"Ah," Benjamin said, nodding. "Now I understand."

"I knew the jury would find him guilty," Athena said. "The evidence against him was overwhelming. My only recourse was to tamper with the jurors so he would be set free for me to deal with as I deem most fitting."

"So you sent notes to each of us promising to pay a thousand dollars if we voted not guilty," Beckman said.

Athena nodded. "And to persuade the other jurors to vote not guilty, as well. My plan worked wonderfully."

"Why just the five of us?" Webber asked. "Why not offer money to all the jurors?"

"The more of you I contacted, the greater the chance one might refuse and report the tampering to the judge. I did not want a mistrial called."

"So you pulled our five names out of hat?" Hurst said with a snicker.

"Hardly," Athena said. "I investigated the backgrounds of everyone on the jury and then chose those mostly likely to take the bait." She showed her teeth in a dazzling smile. "The five of you."

"Come now," Phillip Monroe said. "I'm hardly poor. To me a thousand dollars is a rather small sum."

"True," Athena conceded, "but you love to gamble, and a thousand dollars can buy a lot of chips." She indicated Hurst. "With you it was a simple case of greed."

"I resent that."

"Why resent the truth?" Athena responded. "A friend of yours made the comment that you would beat your own mother if she owed you a dollar and failed to pay it back on time."

"Who the hell told you that lie?" Hurst came out of his chair and leaned toward her, and suddenly the giant in the black jacket and pants was next to him, a huge hand on his shoulder, pushing him back down into his chair. Hurst seemed shocked by the giant's strength.

"Thank you, Largo," Athena said. "Mr. Hurst, I would advise you to control that temper of yours."

Benjamin did not like how her protector raked the five of them with what he would describe as a look of contempt. "Well, you can't say you didn't get your money's worth, Miss Borke. The accused is now a free man, and you're free to have his throat slit or his brains blown out."

"Haven't you been listening?" Athena asked. "Where is the suffering in deaths so quick? Where is the misery? No, the vengeance I have in store for Zachary King is much more refined. Much more thorough."

Theodore Beckman pushed his spectacles up on his nose. "An eye for an eye, is that what you want?"

"Oh, much more than that." Athena smiled. A smile so cold, so wicked, it did not bode well for the object of her hatred. "His very soul for an eye would be more appropriate."

"Enough of this small talk," Hurst said gruffly. "All I care about is the thousand dollars you promised. Hand over the money, lady, so we can get the hell out of here."

"Yes," Phillip Monroe said. "I would like to take my money and go, too."

Athena smiled that same cold smile. "Very well. Largo, would you be so kind as to dispense what each of these gentlemen deserve?"

Benjamin watched the giant move to a shadowed corner and bend over a bench. A large cobweb hung above it. "Is this your house?" he asked. "It certainly doesn't look lived in."

"I rented it under an assumed name," Athena revealed, "and wore a disguise so the landlady cannot identify me later."

"You've covered your tracks admirably," Webber told her.

Athena dipped her shapely chin in acknowledgment of the compliment. "Thank you. There are a few loose ends to tie up and then I can get on with the business of turning Zach King's life into a nightmare."

Largo returned bearing five objects in his hands. He went from one of them to the next, placing an object on the table, then moved to his original position between them and the stairs.

Ira Benjamin stared in disbelief at the Bowie knife. "What in the world is this for?"

"You may use it to protect yourself," Athena said. "It was Largo's idea. He needs the practice. Had it been up to me, I would simply have had him shoot you and be done with it."

"Shoot us?" Beckman said in alarm. "But what

about the thousand dollars you promised in your note?"

"I paid a woman to write them, actually," Athena said, "so the handwriting wouldn't match my own. Then I had Largo snap her neck and left her lying in a ditch."

Hurst was on his feet again. "You're stark raving mad! You can't get away with something like this!"

"On the contrary." Athena stood and backed up near the wall. "I suggest you pick up your knives, gentlemen. Largo is ready to begin."

Benjamin looked. Her bodyguard had not one but two Bowies in his huge hands and was advancing on them in a pantherish crouch. "Please. We'd never tell anyone that you bribed us."

"I must make sure of that." Athena said.

Largo darted forward. Benjamin tried to push his chair back and rise, but he pushed too hard and his chair crashed to the floor, spilling him. He rolled to his knees in time to see Largo nearly decapitate Theodore Beckman with one stroke of a Bowie while simultaneously burying the other knife in Hurst's ample stomach. Largo gave a powerful wrench, and Hurst's internal organs oozed out.

Webber tried to fight and was dispatched with ridiculous ease.

At that point Phillip Monroe broke and ran for the stairs.

Benjamin did the same. They stood no chance against so formidable an adversary. He glanced back and saw that Largo wasn't giving chase, and he smiled, thinking they would escape with their lives.

Then the giant's arms flashed, and twin blades of steel cleaved the air. Benjamin saw Phillip Monroe pitch forward with a Bowie imbedded to the hilt between his shoulder blades even as an acute burning sensation lanced through him and he realized in a burst of raw horror that a Bowie knife was imbedded in his own back. He was vaguely aware of striking the floor, and of pain, and of a voice that came as if from a great distance.

"You know what to do. The kerosene is upstairs. Douse them good. The authorities must not identify the bodies."

"Yes, my mistress."

"And Largo?"

"Yes, mistress?"

"Well done."

The next instant Ira Benjamin's world blinked out of existence.

Chapter Two

Zachary King opened his eyes and was back in the stockade at Fort Leavenworth. He saw the ugly cell bars and smelled the rank, dank odors. He felt the bruises from the beatings and the gnawing pit of hunger in his stomach because he refused to eat the slop they fed him. Panic seized him until there was a light snore. Zach rolled onto his back and beheld the woman he loved more than anything in the world, and he smiled.

Life was deliciously sweet. Zach was free, he was with Louisa, he could go where he wanted, he could do as he pleased. But all he had done since the verdict was rendered two days ago was make up for lost time with his wife. Forty-eight straight hours in bed. He was blissfully relaxed, and more content and at peace with himself than he could ever remember being.

Lou stirred but did not awaken.

Leaning over, Zach lightly nipped her shoulder, then ran a hand from the nape of her neck down her back to the swell of her pert buttocks.

"That tickles."

"Good morning, wench," Zach bantered, and snuggled closer, his arm around her bosom.

"Is that what it is? I've lost track." Lou opened her deep blue eyes and languidly stretched. "I could go on like this forever."

"Or until we starve to death." Zach kissed her neck and pressed his cheek to hers. "Me, I'd like to get up and about."

Lou clasped his arm tight. "I swear," she said in mock indignation. "You don't have a romantic bone in your body."

"Tell that to the nine children we'll have one day."

"Nine? I'd settle for one," Lou wistfully remarked. "I'm surprised we haven't had one already, as randy as you get."

"Me?" Zach playfully tickled her ribs. "You're the one who can't keep her hands off me every hour of the day and night. And here I thought women were supposed to be shy about things like that."

"Every woman has a wildcat inside just busting to get out. All it takes is the right man."

They cuddled a while, until Zach pulled back and asked, "What would you like to do today? And don't reach under the sheet. After being cooped up in that stockade, I need to get out and about."

"I declare," Lou said, "I never thought I would see the day when a male would rather do something other than make love. Some folks say that's all men ever think about."

"I bet all those folks are women," Zach countered, and rolled out of bed to avoid a playful swat. "What is this town like? Kansas?"

"Some people call it Kansas City, but it has a lot of growing to do to earn the name." Lou sat up and the sheet slid down around her waist. "It can be pretty lively. A lot of frontiersmen like us pass through. Indians, too. I've seen Pawnees, a few Mandans, Kanzas Indians, some Otoes."

Zach padded to the washbasin and examined himself in the mirror. He was in dire need of a shave. "Where can we buy supplies? I want to head for the Rockies as soon as possible."

"We have a problem in that regard."

Zach splashed water on his face and began brushing his hair with her hairbrush. "Care to enlighten me or should I guess?" His razor and comb were back in their cabin in the mountains.

"We have four dollars to our name," Lou said as she slid out of bed and began hastily slipping into her buckskins and moccasins. "I'm paid up on this apartment until the end of the week. But we owe legal fees. And when I arrived, I opened an account at a store down the street and we owe six dollars there, too."

"Damn." Zach had never been in debt before. His parents taught him to pay for everything with hard cash or coin so he was never beholden to anyone. Now he understood why. "We can't leave until we pay everything off."

"Stanley P. Dagget said we can take our time and pay him in installments if we want," Louisa said, referring to their lawyer. "I didn't cotton to him much at first, but he's as fine as they come."

"He saved my hash," Zach admitted. Were it not for Dagget, he'd have dangled from the end of a rope by now. "I still can't believe he convinced a jury of white men I was innocent."

"There you go again," Lou scolded. "Just because someone has white skin doesn't mean they hate you." She held her arm out and rolled back the sleeve. "Or haven't you noticed the color of mine?"

Zach laughed and came over and hugged her. "Want to know something? Until I met you I didn't think highly of whites. Most looked down their nose at me because of my mixed blood. Because

I'm part white, part Shoshone." He searched for his buckskins and found them at the foot of the bed. "There were exceptions. My pa, naturally. Shakespeare McNair, Scott Kendall and a few others. But not enough to convince me whites were worth a damn until you came along."

Lou was at the mirror, fussing with her short sandy hair. "There's a lot of hate on both sides. As for me, I can't help it if my kisses are irresistible."

"Don't flatter yourself," Zach said with a huge grin. "I kissed plenty of girls before you came along, and yours weren't anything special."

"Oh, is that right?" Lou took a diving leap and tackled him about the waist. They spilled onto the bed, laughing merrily, and grappled to see who could pin the other. Zach won and claimed his prize by kissing her full on the lips. "Mmmmmm. Not bad," he said. "A little more practice and you'll be as good as my horse."

"Your *horse*!" Lou squealed, and when he cackled, she pushed him clear off the end of the bed onto the floor. "That's the last kiss you'll get today, buster."

Zach lay there admiring the flush of red in her cheeks and the fire in her eyes. "God, you're beautiful."

"And you, sir, are the handsomest devil I know," Lou said. "Now finish getting ready so we can go eat. I'm famished."

"Four dollars won't buy us much." Zach shrugged into his buckskin shirt, tugged on his pants, and bent to pull his moccasins from under the bed. "Maybe we should rent a horse and go off into the hills. We'll shoot a deer and have enough meat to last us a month if we dry and salt it."

"I'd rather splurge at a restaurant I know of," Lou said, cupping her hands in appeal. "Please. It's the first thing we've done since the trial and I want it to be special."

"Women," Zach teased, and then became serious. "I wonder why my parents weren't there. Shakespeare went to fetch them."

"I worry about them, too," Louisa said. "If it was humanly possible, they'd have shown up. I hope— I pray—nothing happened to them."

"That makes two of us."

Pedestrians, carriages and riders thronged the street. Kansas was a town near to bursting at the seams. It had the distinction of growing faster in the past two years than any town on the frontier.

Not all that long ago the press of people would have bothered Zach. Especially the press of so many white people. But now he didn't mind at all. Sure, they were white, but as his father and Lou so often asserted—and as the twelve jurors had proven—not all whites were bigots. The jury had shown him, once and for all, that hating whites on general principle was misguided.

Lou clung to his arm, grinning. "I'm as happy as a pig in mud right about now."

"Just so you don't eat like one at the restaurant," Zach said, and received a jab in the ribs.

Several other couples and an elderly man were quietly eating. The waiter, Zach noticed with a tweak of resentment, seated them in a far corner away from the windows and the entrance. Zach decided not to say anything. Lou was in a good mood and he did not want to spoil it.

They placed their order. Zach was sipping from a glass of water when a mousey little man in a frumpy suit and a bowler entered and came straight for their table. "Mr. and Mrs. King?"

"One of them, anyway," Lou said.

The mousey man was confused. "I beg your pardon?"

"Zach's parents are also Mr. and Mrs. King," Lou clarified, and grinned. "How might we help you?"

"I'm Clarence Potts, a reporter for the *Kansas Sun*. I spotted you on the street, and I would very much like to interview your husband about the trial and its aftermath for the paper."

The water in Zach's mouth turned bitter. Swallowing, he said, "There's nothing more I can say."

"On the contrary," Potts said, and without being asked, he dragged a chair from a nearby table over to theirs, and sat. "Our readers would love to hear your view of the outcome, and how you will deal with any repercussions."

"What are you talking about? Repercussions?" Zach wasn't fond of reporters. They would do anything for a scoop, and half the time their accounts were skewed or outright wrong.

Clarence Potts cleared his throat. "For instance, do you feel justice was served by the verdict of not guilty?"

"Of course." That had to be the stupidest question Zach had ever been asked.

"Really?" Potts took out a pencil and pad. "Some people think the trial was a travesty. That the only reason you were let off is because the government doesn't want trouble with the Shoshones."

Lou was frowning. "That's ridiculous. My husband was found innocent because the jury felt the killings were justified."

Potts scribbled a note, then said, "A lot of people disagree. Or haven't you seen the letters to our editor we've printed? There's even been talk that since the law failed to work as it should, some of our citizens should take it into their own hands."

"Leave," Zach said.

"Another minute or two. I only want to get your side." Potts was scribbling furiously, although what he could be writing, Zach had no idea. "It might help soothe ruffled tempers and show everyone you're not the heartless murderer most believe you to be."

"I won't tell you again."

"Be reasonable, Mr. King. Whether you like it or not, you're news. Big news. The trial hasn't ended your notoriety. Wherever you go from now on, you'll be remembered as the murderous half-breed who escaped the hangman because—"

Zach was out of his chair and had his hands on the reporter's jacket before Potts could blink. Pulling him out of the chair, Zach propelled him toward the entrance, saying, "Enough! If you show your weasel face anywhere near me again, I'll show you just how violent us *breeds* can be." Opening the door, he shoved and sent the reporter stumbling.

The other diners were staring but Zach didn't care.

"What good did that do?" Lou asked as he sat back down.

"Don't start."

"I'm sorry. But this affects me, too. People believe what they read. That reporter might have swayed their opinion by showing you in a favorable light."

Zach snorted. "Don't kid yourself. He was out to paint me as a bloodthirsty savage. He wants to stir people up, not calm them down."

"You're jumping to conclusions." Louisa put her hand on his. "Promise me you won't do anything like that again."

"You heard what the fool said." But to pacify her, Zach added, "I give you my word I won't scalp him or any other reporter unless you say I can. How would that be?"

Lou laughed and patted his arm. "That's a start. But I'm serious. There's no telling how long it will take to pay off our debts and save enough money for the supplies and animals we need, so we should try to get along."

"If you say so." But it had been Zach's experience that getting along with some people was impossible. Their hatred was too deeply ingrained, their bigotry as much a part of them as their hands or feet.

The meal came sooner than Zach expected. The reason became apparent when he cut into his steak. It was almost raw. The potato was undercooked, the soup tepid. He had half a mind to send it back but since Lou was eating without complaint, he controlled his temper.

The meal left them two dollars and five cents to their name.

Lou clasped his arm and strolled cheerfully at his side, going on and on about how much she looked forward to returning home. Zach couldn't stop thinking about Clarence Potts. He wouldn't put it past the man to follow them to their apartment. Some reporters were as single-minded as wolverines when it came to hunting down newsworthy stories.

Accordingly, Zach casually glanced over his shoulder now and then. There was no sign of Potts, but he soon began to suspect someone else was shadowing them.

A block back was a tall man in a brown wide-brimmed hat. He had bushy sideburns and a ruddy complexion—and he never took his eyes off them. Twice Zach stopped at store windows, once to admire a rifle, the second time so Lou could coo over a dress she fancied, and each time the tall man in the brown hat stopped and waited for them to go on.

When he was sure it wasn't his imagination,

Zach turned to Lou. "I'd like to stretch my legs a while if that's all right with you."

"Sure," Lou said. "There's a park up the street from our apartment. Four acres of grass and trees, and a pond. I've been there a few times."

"Sounds perfect," Zach said.

The man in the brown hat stayed a block back the whole way there.

Ducks were paddling about in the pond. It reminded Zach of the high country, of the lake near the cabin where he had been raised in the Rockies. A path led around it into a strip of woodland. As soon as they came to a spot where the vegetation hid them from view, Zach pulled Lou into the undergrowth and crouched. "Get down."

"What in the world are we doing?" Lou whispered.

"Springing a surprise."

Around the bend came the man in the brown hat. His jacket was open, and he had one hand on a pistol tucked under his belt.

Chapter Three

"Are we there yet?" young Evelyn King asked.

Shakespeare McNair twisted in his saddle and regarded her with wry amusement. A white-haired mountaineer who was one of the first to venture west of the Mississippi, he wore fringed buckskins decorated with beads, made by his Flathead wife, Blue Water Woman, the third member of their little party. He had a Hawken rifle in his left hand and a brace of flintlock pistols around his waist. A possibles bag, powder horn, and ammo pouch were angled across his chest. "Do you see a town anywhere?"

"No," Evelyn admitted. She was pushing thirteen but going on twenty. "I'm just worried about my brother, is all."

"Most worthy madam," Shakespeare quoted his namesake, "your honor and your goodness is so evident, that your free undertaking cannot miss a thriving issue." He paused. "We'll get there in time. Don't fret."

"I can't help it," Evelyn said. "The man at that trading post said Zach might be hanged."

"Oh. Him." Shakespeare muttered something, then said, "His brain is as dry as the remainder biscuit after a voyage. He takes false shadows for true substances."

"In other words," said Blue Water Woman, "my husband thinks the man at the trading post talked too much." Her English was exceptional, as was the dignity in her bearing, and her gorgeous features. Streaks of gray lent the elegance of age.

"How do you understand him when he quotes like that?" Evelyn asked. "Half the time I'm not sure what he's saying."

"After all these years," Blue Water Woman

replied, "I have heard most of his quotes many times over."

"Blackguard," Shakespeare said gruffly. "I only repeat myself but once or twice a year." He winked at Evelyn. "I can't help it if certain women don't recognize great literature when they hear it."

"Why Shakespeare?" Evelyn asked.

"Why what?"

"Why did you read all those plays and memorize them? It seems like a terrible lot of trouble to go through just so you can talk like they did in the old days."

Blue Water Woman laughed. "Out of the mouths of children."

Shakespeare pretended to be flustered but answered the girl in earnest. "I was new to the mountains, little one. In the winter there wasn't much to do so I took to reading anything and everything I could get my hands on. A lot of us trappers did in those days. The Rocky Mountain College, we called it. We'd sit around the lodge reading and talking about what we'd read. Or arguing, more often than not."

"My dad did that, too," Evelyn said. "It's how he learned to love books so much."

Shakespeare nodded. "And how I learned to love old William S. You see, one winter I was desperate for something new to read, and another trapper told me about this missionary who had a lot of books. The man of cloth was on his way to the Oregon Country but didn't make it over the Divide before the snows hit. So he built himself a dugout and settled in to wait for the passes to clear."

"You went to see him?"

"He had more books than I ever saw outside of a library. A whole chest full. Homer. Plutarch. Herodotus. Plato. *The Decline and Fall of the Roman Empire*. And a copy of *The Complete Works of William Shakespeare*."

"I bet you talked him into giving it to you. My pa says you can talk the stink out of a skunk."

"He what?" Shakespeare muttered some more, then said, "You would think I'd asked that parson to part with his teeth. I offered him thirty dollars, then fifty, then sixty, and finally he gave in." Reaching back, Shakespeare patted a parfleche. "Ever since, I take it with me practically everywhere I go."

"But why that one book?" Evelyn's innate curiosity wasn't satisfied. "Why not the book on Plato? Or any of those others?"

"That's easy, girl. I wanted my money's worth and it was one of the biggest." Shakespeare's gaze turned inward and backward in time. "Once I started reading it, I couldn't stop. I'd never read anything like old William S. Never heard words used the way he uses them. I took to quoting him, and before I knew it, the other trappers were calling me Shakespeare."

"It's a good thing you didn't pick that Plutarch guy. Plutarch McNair would sound sort of funny."

"I like Homer McNair," Blue Water Woman commented.

They were following a rutted road up a hill. Parked at the summit was a wagon, and seated with his back to a nearby tree was a broomstick in overalls with a floppy hat pulled low over his eyes.

Drawing rein, Shakespeare said, "A fine good morning to you, sir."

The broomstick didn't respond.

"I was wondering if you would be kind enough to tell us how far we are from the town of Kansas?"

"Go away."

"That's not very friendly," Shakespeare observed.

A spindly arm rose and pushed the floppy hat back. "Didn't you see me restin' here? Wakin' me up wasn't friendly, neither."

"As fast locked up in sleep as guiltless labor when it lies starkly in the traveler's bones, he will not wake," Shakespeare quoted.

"Huh?" the man said.

"That was William S."

"Are you a foreigner?" the man asked.

"Do I look like one?" Shakespeare retorted. "All I want to know—"

"You already said," the man snapped. "Skedaddle. I don't make a habit out of talkin' with idiots."

Shakespeare took exception to the insult. "Now see here—"

"No, *you* see," the man curtly interrupted. "That is, if you've got eyes in your head." And he pointed east.

Less than a quarter of a mile from the base of the hill flowed a river, and less than a quarter of a mile beyond the river lay their destination, an oasis of civilization and order in the midst of vast woodland and fertile fields.

"By my troth," Shakespeare declared. "Another ten years and it will rival St. Louis."

"How do we get across the river?" Evelyn wondered.

Snickering, the man by the tree said, "That's why ferries were invented, missy." With that he pulled his hat brim low, folded his arms, and gave a contented sigh.

They were halfway down the hill when Evelyn asked, "Why didn't we ask him about Zach? Maybe he's heard something about the trial."

"We'll find someone less full of himself," Shakespeare said.

A sign read: *McCOY'S FERRY. Est. 1826. Horsepowered flatbed. Safest on the river. Passengers, 10 cents. Horses, mules, oxen, asses, and cows, 15 cents. Calves and colts half price. One-horse carriage, 75 cents. Two-horse wagon, $1.25. Twenty sheep for one dollar. Twenty pigs for two dollars. You clean any mess. Lumber, $1.50 per hundred board feet.* Below, as if an afterthought, someone had written: *Chickens and ducks, fifty cents a dozen. Dogs and cats, five cents.* Below that, in small writing, was: *No free rides. No refunds. No drinking. No spitting. No throwing rocks. No pulling on the ropes. No diving or swimming. No pissing in the river. No use of chamber pots while crossing.*

"Well now," Shakespeare said. "That there is

some sign. I'd say the owner has covered everything."

"Would someone really use a chamber pot with
other people watching?" Evelyn whispered.

"You would be surprised at the things people
will do," Shakespeare said. "There's no end to
their lunacy."

Half the ferry space was filled by a Conestoga
and a smaller wagon and their teams. Wiping his
dirty hands on homespun pants, a middle-aged
man with a chest as big around as a barrel and
arms as thick as stout limbs came over. "I gather
the three of you want to cross?"

Shakespeare nodded. "You take it correctly."

"I always wait until I'm full up, which could be
an hour or more." The ferryman nodded at a cabin.
"My wife sells pretzels, pie and Monogahela, if
you're partial to any or either."

"I haven't had a pie in a coon's age," Shakespeare said. "I just might take you up on that.
How about you ladies?" When Evelyn eagerly
nodded, Shakespeare dismounted and walked his
white mare over and looped the reins around a
hitch rail.

Off in the shade stood four dusty horses tended
by a lanky boy of fifteen or so, his face sprinkled
with freckles. He beamed at Evelyn, revealing a
gap where two of his upper teeth had been.
"Howdy, missy. I'm Charley Varner. I don't recol-
lect ever seein' you in these parts."

Evelyn carefully swung down. "I live in the
Rockies."

"No joshin'?" Charley started toward them but then glanced at the cabin door and stayed where he was. "My pa is always talkin' about goin' there some day, but I doubt we ever will. We just got back from a couple of months out on the prairie lookin' for a spot to farm."

"Out on the prairie?" Shakespeare said.

"Sure. There are eight or ten farms along the Platte already, and my pa says there will be a lot more before too long."

Shakespeare frowned. "So it's begun." He worked the latch on the cabin door and had to stoop to enter, then held the door open for his wife and Evelyn. Tables were against the left wall. Along the right ran a counter. A plump woman with red cheeks was behind it, carving a pie.

"Hurry it up," said one of three men at a table. "We ain't eaten all day and my stomach is growlin'." He had a scraggly beard and wore clothes that had not been touched by water since Noah's flood.

"Hold your horses, mister," the ferryman's wife said. "This just came out of the oven and it's hot."

Crossing the dirt floor, Shakespeare placed his Hawken on top of the counter. "I hope there's more where that came from. I could eat a whole pie all by my lonesome." He noticed that the three men were staring at Blue Water Woman and Evelyn.

"There's four more in the oven," the woman said. "One for you and slices for the ladies?"

"A slice for him, too," Blue Water Woman amended.

The man with the scraggly beard nudged one of

his companions, then said to Shakespeare, "Say, old-timer. They wouldn't happen to be your missus and your sprout, would they? You look a little long at the tooth to be plantin' seeds."

Shakespeare turned, and as he did he shifted his Hawken so the muzzle was pointed at their table. "I shall laugh myself to death at this puppy-headed monster," he quoted. "A most scurvy monster. I could find it in my heart to beat him."

"What did you say?"

"It was from *The Tempest* by William Shakespeare. Maybe you've heard of it?" Shakespeare's query met with blank expressions. "I thought as much. Culture is to clods as rocks are to water."

"You talk damned peculiar," the man said.

"And you would be Mr. Varner, would you not?"

Varner's chin fell to his chest. "How in blazes did you know that? I've never set eyes on you before."

"We spoke to your son outside," Shakespeare enlightened him. "As I understand it, farming has become all the rage west of the Missouri."

"Not yet, but it will, and I'll be one of the first," Varner said. "I'll stake me out a farm as big as Rhode Island and grow more crops than I know what to do with."

"Why Rhode Island when New York and Pennsylvania are so much bigger?"

Varner tilted his head. "I can't decide if you're bein' friendly or insultin' me."

Shakespeare gave a slight bow. "Peace, good tickle brain. I but joust with you over your affront to my manhood."

"Mister, you should be locked away with those people who talk to trees and such," was Varner's considered opinion. "Poke fun at me again and you'll regret it."

"This is strange," Shakespeare quoted. "Methinks my favor here begins to warp."

The ferryman's wife took a large wooden tray crammed with plates and slices of pie to Varner's table. "Here you go. There's plenty more, and bug juice my husband makes to wash it down."

"Bring a jug," Varner said. "Since we can't drink while we're crossin', we might as well wet our throats before we board."

The aroma from the pie had Shakespeare's mouth watering. "Unless my nose is mistaken, that's blackberry," he said as the woman came back around the counter.

"Five cents a slice."

Shakespeare opened his possible bag and took out his poke and laid out the necessary coins.

"Hey, old-timer!" Varner called to him. "Bring your family over here and join us. A grizzled he-bear like you must have seen a lot of this country and must know some prime spots to farm."

"Thank you, but no," Shakespeare said, moving toward a table in the corner where they could eat in peace.

"You're too good for us? Is that it?"

"Don't put words in my mouth, friend." Shakespeare held out a chair for Blue Water Woman. As she sat, she whispered in his ear.

"Watch yourself, husband. There will be trouble."

Shakespeare agreed, which was why he sat with his back to the wall.

The ferryman's wife brought their slices of pie and three forks. She also took a jug to Varner, who uncorked it and gulped, dribbling whiskey down his chin and neck. Smacking his lips, he glanced at them.

Evelyn forked pie into her mouth with relish. "This is delicious. The only thing that would make it better is a glass of milk."

"I'll see if they have any," Shakespeare offered, but just then Varner stood and came over and thrust the jug at him. "What is this?" Shakespeare asked.

"What does it look like?" Varner rejoined. "Take a swig or else."

"Or else what?"

"I'll break your white-haired old neck."

Chapter Four

The tall man in the brown hat had gone a couple of steps past where Zach and Lou were concealed when Zach silently glided onto the footpath and demanded, "Why are you following us?"

The man whirled. His hand tightened on the pistol tucked under his belt, but he didn't draw it. His eyes flicked from Zach to Lou, who had emerged from hiding, then back to Zach again. "What are you talking about?"

Up close, Zach saw that the pistol was a large-caliber pepperbox. He, on the other hand, had no weapons. Not even a knife. The army had confiscated them when he was taken into custody. After the trial he had asked to have them returned, but no one seemed to know where they were. "Who are you, and why have you been shadowing us?"

"Friend, you're imagining things. I come here every day to stretch my legs."

"Liar."

"Believe what you want," the man said, "but you can't go around jumping out at folks or you're liable to be shot." For emphasis he patted the pepperbox. Then he slowly backed away. "Better keep a leash on your husband, lady. He's a few bales shy of a wagon load."

Zach let the man turn and walk off. But as soon as he had gone around the next bend, Zach grabbed Lou's hand and plunged in amid the undergrowth.

"What are we doing? Maybe he was telling the truth."

"Then how did he know you're my wife?"

"Could he be a vigilante?"

"That's what we are going to find out." Zach moved faster, threading through the brush with deceptive ease. He had a lifetime spent in the wilderness to thank. Masters of the craft taught him how to stalk and hunt at an early age, skills he had honed until he was second to none.

The man in the brown hat walked briskly, casting repeated glances over his shoulder. The footpath brought him to a small wooden bridge across a stream. He looked both ways to ensure no one was around, then moved into high weeds along the bank, drew the pepperbox, and crouched.

"He's waiting to see if we're trailing him," Lou whispered.

Zach nodded. They were thirty feet from the bridge, hunkered in a thicket. Their buckskins blended so perfectly into the background, they were invisible. "He doesn't take chances, this one."

"I wish we had my guns. I shouldn't have left them at the apartment," Lou said.

"How were you to know something like this would happen?"

The man in brown watched the footpath. After a while he straightened, wedged the pepperbox under his belt, and crossed the bridge in long strides. He was going somewhere in a hurry.

Zach waited until his quarry was out of sight, then he and Lou crossed the bridge and plunged into the vegetation. It did not take them long to catch up. Presently they reached the end of the park. There, the man moved off along a narrow side street. Zach stayed well back, hugging the buildings. He contrived to keep other pedestrians between them, so when the man in the brown hat slowed and looked back, as he did several times, they weren't spotted.

"He's heading for the center of town," Lou said. "A few more blocks and we'll be near the courthouse."

Images of the trial filled Zach's mind. Of being painted as a cold-hearted murderer by the prosecution. Of hearing the prosecuting attorney tell the jury he deserved to be strung up by the neck and hung until he was dead, dead, dead. Of the hostility of many of the spectators.

Now this.

Zach wondered if Lou was right and the man was one of those who thought he had been wrongly set free. That reporter, Clarence Potts, claimed there were people thinking of taking the law into their own hands.

"He's turning," Lou said.

The man had gone down another street. Zach doubled his pace so as not to lose him, but when he came to the intersection, their quarry was nowhere to be found.

"Where did he get to?"

Zach's natural instinct was to run but instead he went slower. The man might have stepped into a store or a restaurant, of which there were several on both sides of the street.

The first store, though, was a millinery, which catered exclusively to women. The next was a butcher shop, its door wide open, the odor of meat and blood wafting from within.

An elderly woman hobbled toward them using a cane. Her face was pinched like a prune and she gritted her teeth as she walked.

Zach stepped aside so the woman could pass but Louisa surprised him by taking hold of the woman's spindly arm and smiling sweetly.

"Pardon me, ma'am. But did you see a man in a brown hat and jacket go by?"

"Who wants to know?" The old woman fixed a hawkish stare on Zach. "And who is this with you?"

"My husband, ma'am."

"He a redskin?"

Zach clarified things. "My mother is Shoshone. My father is white."

"I don't like redskins," the woman said. "They killed my grandparents. Carved them into pieces, those red devils did, and scalped my grandfather besides."

"I'm sorry," Lou sympathized.

"I wouldn't throw a rope to a drowning redskin," the woman declared. "It would serve the heathens right if we wiped out every last one. Better for the rest of us, I say, and good riddance."

Lou tried again. "A man in brown? Have you seen him?"

"No sir, I surely don't like redskins," the woman said to Zach. "But you, on the other hand," and her tight mouth tweaked in what might be a smile, "you remind me of my second oldest daughter. Melissa, God rest her soul. The consumption took her. She was only twenty-four. Wasted away right before my eyes and there wasn't a thing I could do."

"Losing a loved one is always hard," Lou said. "I lost my mother and father."

"Melissa was my favorite. She never sassed me,

never gave me a lick of trouble. But God took her anyway." The woman's pinched features pinched even more. "This life makes no sense. Why let us be born only to die? Why let us taste happiness only to suffer?"

"The man in brown?" Lou prompted.

"My own days will end soon. I'm not long for this world, and I'll go out knowing as little as when I came in. Sorrow and misery, that's our lot in life. Sorrow and misery and a grin now and then." The woman hobbled on, a tear trickling down her right cheek. She went a short way, then stopped and pointed with her cane. "The fellow you want went there."

"Thank you," Lou said.

It was a tavern called The Tankard. Zach drew Lou across the street and into a nook between buildings. "Wait here."

"Not on your life. Whatever this is about, we'll see it through together."

Zach refused to budge when she tugged on his sleeve. "A tavern is no place for a woman. I've never been in one but that's what my father has told me. You go in there, you draw attention to us."

"What if it's a trap? What if he's on to us and he jumps you? I can't help if I'm way over here."

"The first hint of trouble, I'll come back out." By then it might be too late, but Zach would cross that stream when he came to it.

"I'll give you five minutes, then I'm coming in," was the most Lou would allow.

Zach hurried across. He slowly opened the door,

making it a point to stand to one side so he wouldn't be silhouetted against the sunlight. Taking a couple of steps, he paused to give his eyes time to adjust. He smelled the urine-like odor of beer, familiar from his visits to the rendezvous of yesteryear, and the pungent odor of tobacco.

The bar was to Zach's right, tables were straight ahead, booths were to his left. A lone lamp provided the only light. The bartender was playing dice with a pair of men with bellies as big as clothes baskets. Several booths were occupied, but all Zach could see was the tops of heads. None of them wore a brown hat.

Zach slid into the first booth. He wondered if the man in brown had spotted him and slipped out the back. No sooner did the thought cross his mind than the man came out of a hall at the far end of the room and walked to the bar.

Zach placed his elbow on the table and bent forward so his arm partially hid his face. He need not have worried; the man never looked his way.

Taking a stool at the bar, the man ordered a drink. He took out a pocket watch and checked the time, then set the open watch in front of him.

Waiting for someone, Zach guessed. He had an urge to go over and confront him but the man had a gun and he didn't.

A barmaid appeared from out of the back, spotted him, and walked over smiling. The smile died when she reached the booth. "Well now, look what we have here." In her late thirties or early forties, she had strawberry hair and no waist to speak of.

"Spare us both some grief, kid. The boss doesn't like your kind. You'd better scoot. Two blocks west and one block south is a watering hole that caters to Indians."

"I'm part white," Zach said.

"Maybe so, but you don't much look it, and why ask for a busted lip if you don't want one, eh?" She took it for granted he would leave and turned to walk off.

"Bring me a beer. Any kind will do."

Putting her hands on her hips, the barmaid sighed. "Not big on taking advice, are you? Suit yourself. But don't say I didn't warn you if you get your teeth knocked down your throat."

The man in the brown hat seemed lost in thought. He didn't look up when the barmaid came to the bar. She huddled with the bartender and returned bearing a tray with a mug brimming with beer.

"I hope you choke."

Only then did Zach remember Louisa had their money. But the barmaid didn't ask to be paid. He watched her flounce to another booth and settled back to see what the man in the brown hat did next.

Suddenly light cleaved the room like a golden axe. The bartender and the men with the big bellies glanced sharply at the entrance.

Zach knew who it would be. He rose high enough to see over the top of the booth, and motioned for her to join him. "You didn't wait five minutes."

"I tried. I couldn't." Lou was blinking and squinting. "Why don't they open the curtains? It's darker than a cave."

"You're lucky he didn't see you." Zach pointed at the man in the brown hat, who was nursing his drink and still absorbed in whatever he was thinking about.

Just then the bartender came around the end of the bar and over to their booth. He had brawny arms and knuckles that could double as walnuts and he wasn't in a friendly frame of mind. "Marge tells me she asked you to leave and you wouldn't. Is that right, boy?"

"It's right," Zach said.

"Is there a problem, mister?" Lou asked.

"The name is Treach. I own this place, and I serve who I damn well please. That doesn't in-cludes darkies and it doesn't include Indians." Treach pointedly glared at Zach. "Or breeds, like your boyfriend here."

"He's my husband."

Treach sneered and said, "Do tell. To each their own. But those of us who don't stoop to matin' with animals don't want it rubbed in our faces. Take your hubby and leave, lady, or I'll have the two of you thrown out on your ear."

Lou said, "We don't want any trouble."

"Then you should have had more brains than to marry a half-and-half."

Zach gripped the handle of his mug and envi-sioned mashing it against the tavern owner's face. "Don't talk to my wife like that."

"Or what?" Treach leaned on the table, the muscles in his arms bulging. "Look, boy. I'm tryin' to be polite. I could have taken you by the scruff of your breed neck and tossed you out in the street, but I didn't."

"Please," Lou said.

Treach looked at her, then at Zach. "Finish your beer and go, and you'll make it through the day in one piece."

"I don't like being threatened."

"Some people don't have the brains of a tree stump." Treach straightened, extended an arm, and snapped his fingers. It was a signal for the two men with the big bellies to slide off their stools and waddle to his side.

"Is there a problem?" the one with the biggest belly asked.

"I've got me a mouthy breed who won't heed his betters," Treach said. "I think we should teach him some respect."

"Hold on!" Lou rose and angrily poked him in the chest. "No one is teaching my husband anything. You want us to go, we'll go."

"No," Zach said.

Both Lou and Treach responded at the same moment with, "What?"

"I have as much right to be here as anyone else."

The other big belly chortled. "You've got a lot to learn, fella. This ain't New York or one of those Injun-lovin' places."

Coiling his legs, Zach slid to the edge of the seat.

"I'm sick and tired of being picked on because of the color of my skin. I can't help who I am. I was born this way."

"I'm about to break into tears," Treach said sarcastically. "Either of you boys have a violin?"

"No, but we've got us some fists," said one, slamming his right fist into his left palm. "And we're damn good at usin' 'em."

"What's it goin' to be, breed?" Treach asked. "Easy or hard?"

Lou turned. "Please. Let's just leave."

"Hard," Zach said.

Chapter Five

Shakespeare McNair was a peaceful sort by nature. Given his druthers, he would live in harmony with all men, whether red, white, black or blue. But life seldom let him have his druthers. Life liked to remind him, all too often, that peace and harmony were fine ideals, but the real world was rife with hatred, arrogance and stupidity.

Varner was a living example. He held out the jug with a smug smirk on his bearded face, openly daring Shakespeare to refuse. "Well? What's it going to be? Do you take a sip or not?"

"It's a mistake," Shakespeare said.

"What is?"

"Trying to prove how tough you are by bullying someone who has held his own against Blackfeet and Apaches."

Varner found that humorous. "Big words for an old buzzard. Maybe you were a regular bear of the woods in your younger days, but they're behind you. Now you're nothin' but a windbag."

"Reckon so, do you?" Shakespeare asked, and drove the Hawken's stock into the pit of Varner's stomach. The farmer doubled over, puffing and gurgling while clutching the jug in both hands.

"Let me help you with that." Wresting the jug free, Shakespeare brought it crashing down on Varner's head. Fragments and whiskey flew every which way and Varner collapsed like a poled ox, blood trickling from several cuts. He groaned once and was still.

Shakespeare spun, leveling the Hawken at Varner's friends. "How about you two? Care to waltz?"

"Easy with that rifle, you cantankerous old goat," one said. "He was the one ridin' you, not us."

"Thou hast no more brain than I have in my elbows," Shakespeare quoted.

"Huh? Elbows don't have brains."

"Nor, in your case, does the space between your ears." Shakespeare kept the rifle on them. "I didn't hear you try to stop your friend."

"Sam is a grown man. He digs his own holes. Bill and me, we like to mind our own business."

"That's right!" declared the third man. "Live and

let live, I always say. You've no call to be pointin' that cannon at us."

"How green you are and fresh in this old world." But Shakespeare lowered the Hawken. "All right. You get to live. But I'd as soon shoot you as stomp grapes, so do mind your elders."

"You're plumb crazy," one bleated.

"And your abilities are too infantile for doing much alone." Shakespeare nodded at Varner's prone form. "Drag him out. When he comes to, inform him this was only a warning. Next time I won't be nearly as nice."

Reclaiming his seat, Shakespeare placed the Hawken across his lap and renewed his assault on his slice of blackberry pie. "Thank goodness the clod hasn't spoiled my appetite."

Blue Water Woman did not look pleased. "Was all that necessary? Or have you become vicious in your old age?"

"Once a man starts backing down, it becomes a habit," Shakespeare said. "I like holding my head high."

Evelyn wasn't the least bit disturbed by the violence. "You're a lot like my pa, Uncle Shakespeare. He never lets anyone push him around, either."

"We're a dwindling breed," Shakespeare said, his mouth full of pie. "Civilization is to blame. When men rely on the law to stand up for them, they forget how to stand up for themselves."

"You don't think much of towns and cities, do you?" Evelyn inquired.

"There's more to it than that. Civilization isn't only buildings and streets. It's how people think."

"They don't think like we do?"

Shakespeare was reminded of when her brother Zach was her age. They were both continual question marks. "Civilized folks live in cages and don't see the bars. From the day they're born, they're taught to always abide by the law. Always be nice. Always bend over backwards to avoid trouble. So when trouble comes, when someone threatens them, they run for the law instead of dealing with it themselves."

"I plan to live in a city one day," Evelyn said.

"Don't remind me," Shakespeare responded crustily. For years she had been saying how much she preferred civilized existence to the wilderness.

Evelyn looked hurt. "Do you hold it against me too? I know my father does. He thinks I'll regret it."

Shakespeare gave her an honest answer. "It's not for me to judge, princess. Lord knows, my life hasn't been perfect. I've made more mistakes than most ten people."

"Would you ever live in a city?"

"Not in a million years." Shakespeare sighed and set down his fork. "But just because I wouldn't do it doesn't mean it's wrong for everyone. A lot of people are perfectly happy living as others tell them to live."

Blue Water Woman laughed. "Pay no attention to him, Evelyn. He is so set in his ways, they are etched in stone."

"I know what I like," Shakespeare conceded,

"and the one thing I like more than anything else in this world is being free. I like doing what I want when I want without someone looking over my shoulder. I won't abide chains, physical or mental."

Evelyn said, "A city isn't a chain."

"Isn't it?" Shakespeare argued. "In a city you have to wear certain clothes and cut your hair a certain way or people think you're strange. You can't spit or scratch yourself or drink to excess without someone wagging a finger. There are laws on where you can walk and where you can't, laws on how you should behave and how you shouldn't, laws that take your hard-earned money and give it to layabouts who spend it as if money spews from a bottomless geyser."

"You make it sound horrible," Evelyn said, "but the mountains have their bad side. Grizzlies rip people to shreds. Mountains lions and wolves and wolverines are everywhere. Hostiles are always out to count coup." Evelyn ended her litany. "I could say more. But it sure seems to me a person can live a lot longer in a city than in the high country."

Shakespeare had more he could say, too, but he finished the pie. Evelyn was young yet. She had a lot to learn, and the best teacher was life itself. Sometimes it was the *only* teacher.

True to the ferryman's word, within the hour he came in and announced he was ready for them to board.

Varner and his companions already had. Varner

with a visible bump on his head and an ugly scowl on his face. Freckle-faced Charley smiled at Evelyn and was disappointed when she didn't stand next to him.

Shakespeare counted seventeen others. What with their horses and cows and a few pigs and the Conestoga and the other wagon, the ferry was dangerously overloaded, in Shakespeare's estimation. But he was a mountaineer, not a ferryman, so who was he to tell the ferryman how to run the ferry? Still, as the shout was given to cast off and a rope was tugged to signal the other side, his gut bunched into a knot.

"Isn't this grand?" Evelyn's eyes were alight with the grand adventure of it all. "I've never been on a ferry before."

The opposite shore seemed god-awful far to Shakespeare but he blamed that on his frayed nerves. It didn't help that he never learned to swim all that well. Oh, he could manage when he had to, but swimming had never been high on his list of things he most liked to do.

Blue Water Woman couldn't swim a lick yet she was as calm as calm could be, serenely watching the water flow by. "Neither have I, little one," she said to Evelyn. "We share a special moment."

As he regularly did, Shakespeare marveled that so beautiful and intelligent and fine a woman had taken him as her own. Why she loved him and only him, out of all the men she'd ever met, was a never-ending source of mystery and gratitude. Life without her was unthinkable.

The ferry made good headway but the crossing would take considerable time. The ferryman was at one end, his helper at the other. Old hands at this, they kept their eyes on the ropes and their long poles at the ready. Although what good the poles would do, given how deep the river ran, Shakespeare couldn't imagine.

Soon a horse began nickering and prancing and its owner grabbed hold of the bridle to quiet it down.

Blue Water Woman was still staring at the water. Putting an arm across her shoulders, Shakespeare grinned, "A back rub for your thoughts, my lady fair."

"I was thinking how our lives are a lot like this river. Time flows by so fast, we go from cradle to grave before we know it."

Shakespeare watched a piece of driftwood go floating by. Of late he had been thinking a lot about his own mortality. He loved life dearly, but as his white hair attested, realistically he wasn't long for this world. Each new day was a precious gift, made more so by the unavoidable fact that he might not live to see the next. Nate King liked to tease him about it, to say that as healthy and robust as he was, he would live to be as old as Methuselah. But Nate didn't know about the chronic aches in Shakespeare joints and muscles. Nate didn't know that some mornings Shakespeare woke up so stiff he could barely move.

Blue Water Woman was right. Life went by too damn fast. To Shakespeare, it seemed like only yesterday that he was a young buck at his peak, venturing where few whites had ever gone, into the vast unknown west of the mighty Mississippi. Back then he was a fountain of energy. He could hike all day and all night and still not be tired. Old age—and death—had seemed so remote and unlikely as to not be worthy of consideration. Of late that had changed; both weighed heavily, anchors to a reality Shakespeare could no longer deny.

"Oh, look!" Evelyn squealed. "Did you see that?"

A large fish of some kind had leaped clear of the river and splashed back down again.

Shakespeare would give anything to be her age. To have his whole life before him. He sometimes wondered if he had it to do again, would he do it the same? Would he make more of himself? Or would he blunder along much as he had blundered through this life? Swept along on time's currents as that driftwood had been swept along by the river? Like most men, he tended to delude himself that he was master of his own destiny when in truth no one ever was or ever had been or ever would be.

"There's another one!" Evelyn exclaimed.

Shakespeare's hand found Blue Water Woman's, and he gently squeezed. One of his deepest regrets was that they found one another too late in life to have children. He would have liked to have a family of their own, four or five little wild ones to wear them to a frazzle.

Hooves suddenly thudded. The same horse was still acting up despite its owner's best efforts.

"Quiet that animal!" the ferryman bawled.

The ferry was sturdily built. It would take more than a frightened horse to damage it. But Shakespeare grew more and more uneasy the longer the animal reared and kicked. Horses were easily panicked. Spook one, and those around it would catch its fear, like a contagion.

Varner's party was closer and moved to give the horse more room. Young Charley Varner's horse began bobbing its head and whinnying, but he had firm hold of its reins.

Blue Water Woman leaned against Shakespeare and said in a low voice so Evelyn wouldn't hear, "I have been thinking. What if the trial is over and Stalking Coyote was found guilty?"

Stalking Coyote was Zach King's Shoshone name; Evelyn's was Blue Flower. "All we can do is pray he's still with us."

"I would spare Evelyn the pain if I could."

As would Shakespeare. "We'll do what we can if it comes to that."

Out over the river a heron appeared, winging toward the west shore with powerful strokes of its long wings. Shakespeare envied it. Westward lay the Rockies, and home, where he would much rather be. But he had given Nate King his word that he would help Zach, so help him he would.

"Be careful," Blue Water Woman said to Evelyn, who was leaning her head past the top rail.

"I'm just watching a fish."

Shakespeare imagined her falling over the side and disappearing under the surface, and his stomach churned. He almost reached out and yanked her back. But he stopped himself. He was being silly. The rails were there. She was perfectly safe.

"Consarn it!" the ferryman suddenly bellowed. "Can you calm that blasted animal or not!"

The horse that had been causing trouble was causing more. A second man sprang to help its owner, and between them they held it still, though it quaked and whinnied.

Evelyn beckoned. "Uncle Shakespeare! Aunt Blue Water Woman! Come see the pretty patterns!"

The idea of being that near the edge made Shakespeare's gut flip-flop even worse, but since his wife went over, he went over, too. The surface was deceptively placid except where the water disappeared in a rush under the ferry. There, tiny eddies and swirls blossomed like miniature whirlpools.

"Can I dip my fingers in?" Evelyn asked.

"You most certainly can not," Shakespeare said, and placed a hand on her shoulder in case she decided to anyway.

"I just want to feel the water. I bet it tickles."

"You wouldn't touch a porcupine to see if its quills would stick in you," Shakespeare said.

"A river and a porcupine are two different things," Evelyn aptly noted.

A whinny split the air. The horse the two men were holding broke loose and rose onto its hind legs. The men leaped to grab it but were knocked aside by flailing hooves, and the next moment the horse was in among the horses belonging to the farmers. Those horses, in turn, pushed against Shakespeare's white mare and Blue Water Woman's bay. Shakespeare gripped both bridles, saying, "There now. There now."

Confusion reigned. More horses whinnied and plunged. There was a loud *crack*, as of splintering wood, and a scream rang out.

Shakespeare whirled, his blood going cold at the sight of the broken rails—and of Evelyn pitching into the river.

Chapter Six

Zach King couldn't help himself. He hated it when others treated him with contempt for being a "breed." He hated that an accident of birth had branded him for life. He hated it so much that when Treach reached for him, he exploded out of the booth like a bear out of its den, slamming into Treach and rocking him back on his heels.

"Damn you!" Treach regained his balance and raised his fists. "I'll pound you to a pulp!"

Quick as lightning, Zach landed a right uppercut that crunched Treach's teeth together. A left jab and a right cross completed the job and sent Treach crashing to the floor.

By then the two men with big bellies were closing in, their thick fingers hooked into claws to grapple and wrestle.

Zach knew that once they got their hands on him, he was in for it. Skipping right, then left, he punched one in the head. It was like punching an anvil. All the man did was grunt and keep on coming.

"Gonna stomp you, boy. Gonna stomp you good."

The other big belly nodded. "Gonna kick in your teeth and break your fingers. Gonna learn you to do as your betters say."

Zach sidestepped toward the middle of the room so they couldn't trap him against the booths. He dodged a pudgy hand that grabbed at his wrist, evaded a lunge that was laughable. They were big but they were slow, slow of wit as well as reflexes. If he had a gun or a knife they would be lying in pools of blood by now.

But they were not entirely stupid, as they proved by one circling left while the other circled right. They intended to catch him between them, and slow or not, with their greater reach, they just might do it.

Pivoting, Zach darted to one side, narrowly avoiding outstretched hands. In doing so he ended up next to a table. The pair instantly converged. Twisting away, he leaped into the clear. Or so he thought until arms looped around him from behind and Treach growled in his ear.

"Forgot about me, didn't you, breed? Now you bleed!"

The big bellies smiled. "Hold him good!" one said. "We'll break him like a twig."

Zach wrenched first one way, then another, seeking to throw Treach off, but the man had arms of iron. He brought a foot down on Treach's instep and Treach roared in pain and fury but the bands held firm.

Then Louisa was there. "Let my husband go!" she cried, and punched Treach in the face. She was small but she was wiry and her punches were nothing to sneeze at. Treach let go of Zach and staggered, blood oozing from both nostrils. Lou kicked him in the knee, and when he howled and doubled over, she kicked him on the jaw. Down Treach went, to lie as motionless as a log.

One of the big bellies lumbered toward her.

Taking a bound, Zach seized the wrist of the second big belly and whipped the man completely around, slinging him into the one going after Lou. Limbs askew, the pair tumbled. Predictably, they were slow to get to their knees, affording Zach time to slip in and deliver a flurry of precise, rocking blows. Their chins were hard as rock and it hurt his knuckles, but the end result was that both men lay on their big bellies, unconscious.

"You did it!" Lou exclaimed, hugging him.

"We did it," Zach said. None of the other customers had interfered, but he wouldn't put it past them to send for the law, so taking Lou's wrist, he backed toward the entrance. Belatedly, he remembered the man in the brown hat.

The stool the man had been on was empty.

"He saw us and slipped out," Lou read Zach's thoughts.

Together they dashed outside and scoured the street. Zach regretted letting his temper get the better of his common sense. "Now we'll never know who he was or why he was following us."

Louisa shrugged. "Oh well. Let's get out of here before those men inside recover. I've seen enough of cell bars to last me a lifetime."

Her suggestion had merit. They jogged the first few blocks, stuck to a brisk walk thereafter, and reached her apartment without incident. Once inside, Lou molded her body to his.

"I was worried there for a bit. Why did you provoke them like that?"

"What else should I have done? Turned the other cheek?" Zach gazed deep into her eyes. "That's not me. Not my way. My father and mother were always going on and on about how I shouldn't stoop to the level of those who hate me for what I am, but there's only so much a person can take."

"Hasn't the ordeal we've been through taught you anything?" Lou asked. "Fighting hatred with hatred isn't the answer."

"What is, then? To let people like Treach treat me like scum and push me around? Deny I have any pride or dignity?"

"I didn't say that," Lou said.

"You might as well have. A man has to stick up for himself or he can't call himself a man. For years I did as my parents wanted and never lifted a finger. Each time I swallowed an insult, it was like swallowing a bitter root. Each time I kept quiet, I lost a little more respect for myself."

Lou placed her hands on his cheeks. "All I ask is that you be more careful. I came close to losing you to a hangman and I don't want to go through that again."

Zach wished he could make her understand. But only someone who had been through the living hell he had, only someone who had suffered the arrows and barbs of contempt and loathing, ever could. "I'll try," was the best compromise he could make.

Grinning, Lou pushed him toward the bedroom. "Now that that's out of the way, what do you say to a nap?"

"I'm not tired."

"Me either," Lou said, and laughed.

A knock on the door brought them up short. Lou was rooted by indecision but not Zach; he ran to the table and armed himself with her flintlocks. "Who is it?"

"Mr. King? Mr. Zachary King? I would very much like a word with you, if you don't mind."

"You haven't said who you are."

"My name is Wainwright. Mortimer Wainwright. I'm an attorney at law, and I'm here on behalf of a client."

Zach gestured, and Lou went to the door and opened it. The man who entered took one look at the pistols and flung his arms out to either side.

"Don't shoot! I'm not armed! Honest! All I have with me is my valise."

Sliding past him, Zach checked the stairs. Wainwright was alone. He closed the door and stepped back. "Suppose you tell us what you're doing here."

"Gladly," the lawyer said. "But I would be ever so grateful, and much more at ease, if you would lower your weapons and permit me to sit down."

As always, Lou was friendlier than Zach was inclined to be. "You must forgive us, Mr. Wainwright. We've made a few enemies and can't be too trusting."

"Nothing to forgive, my dear." Wainwright wasn't much over five feet tall, his clothes nicely tailored. He was graying at the temples and had a salt-and-pepper mustache and trimmed beard. "In your situation I would feel the same." He chose a chair and rested the valise on his legs. "I apologize for popping in unannounced, but I assure you it's in your best interests to hear me out."

"We'll be the judge of that," Zach said.

Lou gave him what Zach liked to call her "wifely" look, then said to their visitor. "If this is a legal matter you should talk to our lawyer, Stanley Dagget. I can give you his address."

"Oh, it need not concern him, I assure you." Wainwright removed his bowler. "My client specifically requests that we keep this among ourselves."

"Who is this client you keep mentioning?" Zach asked suspiciously. Based on his experience with lawyers, he didn't trust any of them as far as he could heave Pike's Peak.

"I'm not at liberty to say."

Zach snorted and said, "Don't let the door hit you on the ass on your way out."

"Zachary King! That's no way to talk." Lou was embarrassed. Perching on the settee, she addressed their visitor. "Is there a reason your client doesn't want us to know who they are?"

"The best reason in the world, Mrs. King. As you are probably aware, a goodly number of our town's less tolerant citizens don't think highly of your husband. They would as soon he had been sentenced to hang."

"Tell us something we don't know," Zach snapped.

Again Lou gave him "the look," then said to Wainwright, "What does that have to do with your visit?"

"My client prefers no one else learn of it. Should word slip out, the same people who want your husband dead might channel some of their hatred in my client's direction."

Zach grinned. "We wouldn't want that."

Wainwright coughed and continued. "What should concern you most is that my client believes a great injustice has been done. An injustice so severe, it demands redress."

From Lou: "How do you mean?"

"My client would like to extend a small kindness," Wainwright said. "A token to show you that there are people in this world who don't judge others by their race."

"A complete stranger wants to do this for us?" Now it was Lou who was suspicious. "If this is a lark it's in poor taste."

Wainwright started to open the valise and Zach

instantly trained a flintlock on him. "Please, Mr. King. I am not about to commit suicide." Wainwright removed a sheath of bills, counted out a hundred dollars, and gave them to Lou. "My client read about your debts and hopes this will help alleviate them."

"A thousand would alleviate them more," Zach said.

"You're hopeless," Lou chided.

Wainwright chuckled. "That's perfectly all right, Mrs. King. To tell you the truth, your husband is a man after my own heart." To Zach he said, "But a thousand dollars is out of the question. My client's sense of charity only extends so far." He opened the valise again, took out a paper, and handed it to Lou. "This is a receipt for one night's stay at the Armistead Hotel. Perhaps you have heard of it? Over on Fremont Street?"

"It's where all the well-to-do stay," Lou said. "They say the beds have silk sheets and there's a crystal chandelier in the lobby."

"It's the best hotel in town," Wainwright acknowledged. "And you and your husband are booked into one of their best suites, all expenses paid."

"Enough," Zach said. Marching over to the lawyer, he touched the flintlock's muzzle to Wainwright's forehead. "You have ten seconds to tell me what this is really all about."

"Christian charity," was Wainwright's reply. "Plain and simple. My client is a Good Samaritan of the first order. Just last month I gave another hundred dollars to a poor family who lost their meager belongings in a fire. Two months ago my client bestowed a large endowment on an orphanage."

"Then your client does this all the time?" Lou said.

Wainwright nodded. "So you see, there's nothing extraordinary about the offer. It's simply the kind gesture of a generous soul." He folded his hands on the valise. "What will it be? Do you accept? Or should I cancel the reservation and inform my client you've declined?"

Zach expressed his honest sentiments. "I smell fish."

"What can it hurt?" Lou said. "We need the money. And a night at the hotel would be wonderful."

"There's more to it," Zach insisted. "There has to be."

Mortimer Wainwright let out a long sigh. "I don't know what else I can do to convince you of my client's sincerity. But I'll tell you what. Keep the money, and if you don't spend the night at The Armistead, you'll still come out ahead."

"That's sweet of you," Lou said.

"I only want to do what is best for everyone, Mrs. King."

Five minutes later Mortimer Wainwright came down the stairs and turned left. He walked four blocks, stopping frequently to ensure he wasn't followed. At a restaurant on Cavendish Street he took a table near the window and ordered a bowl of soup. He was on his second spoonful when a broad-shouldered giant sank into the chair across from him.

"How did it go?"

"Exactly as she predicted it would, Mr. Largo. The wife was willing, the half-breed was skeptical as hell."

"You carried out my mistress's instructions?"

"I pride myself on my efficiency. I said exactly what she wanted me to say, did exactly what she wanted me to do."

Largo's huge hand slid under his jacket and pulled out an envelope. "Here is the money you were promised. Remember, you must never say a word to anyone." He reached across the table, his hand over the soup.

"I gave my word, didn't I?" Wainwright accepted the envelope and placed it in his valise.

"My mistress asked me to thank you," Largo said. Again he extended his hand over the bowl.

Wainwright shook. "I'm the one who should be grateful. She's paying me more than I normally earn in six months." He spooned some soup into his mouth, and swallowed. "Why did you pick me, if you don't mind my asking?"

"You have no immediate family," Largo said.

"How is that a factor?" Wainwright dipped the spoon into the bowl two more times before the manservant answered.

"No wife. No children. No one to ask questions afterward."

"After what?" Wainwright downed another mouthful, then coughed. "Strange. All of a sudden my throat is burning."

"That's the first sign," Largo said. "Next you'll grow weak. Then you will lose control of your body. I would guess you have approximately twenty-five seconds left to live."

All the color drained from Wainwright and he stood, or tried to, but his legs wouldn't bear his weight. Weakly clutching his throat, he looked in desperation at the other diners and tried to speak but couldn't.

Largo stood, came around the table, and picked up the valise. "My mistress wants her money back."

He was gone from the restaurant when Mortimer Wainwright's face sank into the bowl of soup and stayed there.

Chapter Seven

For a span of heartbeats Shakespeare McNair was paralyzed by fear such as he'd never felt in a long and peril-filled life. Then he let go of the mare and the bay and sprang to the side to save Evelyn. Just as he did, the horses that were acting up pushed against the mare and the bay, forcing them, in turn, to push again him, knocking him off-balance and nearly sending him over the rail.

The ferryman and his helper were bawling for the owners of the frightened animals to get them under control while hurrying to help.

Shakespeare tried to reach the gap where the rail had broken, but the mare had him pinned. He slapped her side, but she was hemmed in by the other horses and couldn't move. In vain he searched the surface of the river, his fear climbing to new heights. But it was nothing compared to the fear that overwhelmed him when a sorrel owned by the Varners shouldered violently against Blue Water Woman. Like him, she was frantically seeking sign of Evelyn, and didn't notice her peril until too late. The impact drove her toward the break through which Evelyn had plunged.

"Grab hold!" Shakespeare cried.

Blue Water Woman tried to grip the rail but couldn't stop her plunge. She fell headfirst into the swirling river. Headfirst, a woman who had never learned to swim and never been in water deeper than her waist.

Pure, total terror gripped Shakespeare. He pushed against the bay, and somehow found the strength to push it away from him this time. Dropping his rifle and flintlocks, he stepped to the break and glanced at the spot where Evelyn had gone under and then at the spot where Blue Water Woman had gone under. He could only save one. *Who would it be?*

God help him, Shakespeare thought, as he tucked and dived. A cold watery fist closed around him. Everything became a blur. He stroked cleanly, rapidly, going deep, afraid he wouldn't find her. Then his left hand made contact with buckskin and he gripped it with all his might, arched his back, and kicked toward the surface.

His lungs were hurting. He had not taken as deep a breath as he should. A shimmering golden glow beckoned, and they broke up into the sun and the air. Shakespeare held Blue Water Woman to him as she coughed and spat out water and clung to his shoulders.

"Evelyn?" she choked out.

Shakespeare felt sick inside. He glanced at the ferry, which had finally come to a stop. The current was carrying them away from it, and he wasn't sure he had the strength left to reach it. Then a rope sailed out of the blue and struck his head and shoulders. Someone hollered for him to hold on, which he did, wrapping it around them both so Blue Water Woman wouldn't slip from his grasp.

The ferryman and the Varners and others began pulling them in. Sam Varner was at the forefront, pulling hardest of all.

"Evelyn?" Blue Water Woman said again, and now she was casting about in wide-eyed panic. She looked at him, and he saw comprehension dawn, and she said softly, "Oh, husband, you didn't."

Shakespeare shriveled inside. "I did what I had to," he answered, but the words were as hollow as the spreading emptiness inside him. He was barely aware of being pulled to the ferry, of strong hands reaching down and lifting, of a blanket being thrown over his shoulders and hands clapping him on the back.

"Thank God you saved her!" the ferryman exclaimed. "I haven't lost anyone in a thousand crossings and I don't want to spoil my record."

Rousing, Shakespeare wanted to grip him by the throat and throttle him silly. "You're forgetting the girl," he said forlornly.

"Hell, she swims like a fish." The ferryman grinned. "She caught hold of the back and was climbing on when you went over the side."

A small hand squeezed Shakespeare's, and he saw Evelyn, all smiles and relief. "Uncle Shakespeare! Blue Water Woman! You had me so scared! I wanted to dive in after you but the man wouldn't let me."

Shakespeare's throat grew tight. He tried to speak but couldn't. Tears misted his eyes, and it felt as if his chest were folding in on itself. It was Blue Water Woman who pulled Evelyn to them, and he hugged them both close to his chest, his heart pounding so loud, he imagined everyone could hear.

Only after the tears stopped and the pounding subsided did Shakespeare wipe his face with a wet sleeve and slowly clamber to his feet. "Thank you for saving us," he said to the ferryman, "and for not letting her jump in."

"I didn't stop her," the ferryman said. "It was him." He nodded at Sam Varner.

Shakespeare's shame was complete. "Thanks." He thrust out his hand and the farmer shook.

"Sorry about back there at the landin', mister. I don't rightly know what got into me."

All Shakespeare could do was nod. He was too choked up to say anything. His whole world was in shambles. Shuffling to a pack, he sat and slumped over, dejected.

The horses were calmed and separated. After the ferryman's helper signaled to shore, the ferry resumed its crawl.

His head in his hands, Shakespeare tried to come to grips with what he had done, and couldn't. Shadows fell across him, but he didn't look up.

"Are you all right, Uncle Shakespeare?" Evelyn asked.

Shakespeare could not say anything.

"All is well," Blue Water Woman said. "Evelyn saved herself, and you saved me. But I am afraid I lost my rifle."

"And I lost mine." Evelyn was particularly sad. "The one Pa had custom made for me by the Hawken brothers."

Shakespeare couldn't bring himself to meet their gaze. Clearing his throat, he managed, "We were lucky. Damned lucky."

"Don't be sad. We're fine now." Evelyn's slim arm looped around his neck, and he wanted to cry. "I was so afraid. I couldn't bear it if something happened to either of you."

Shakespeare groaned and bit his lower lip and inwardly cursed himself for being the vilest man alive.

The rest of the crossing went smoothly. Blue Water Woman led their horses onto shore. Shakespeare glumly followed, Evelyn's hand in his. Every time he looked at her, she smiled. Every time she smiled, he wanted to tear out his eyes.

The ferryman approached. "I need your address."

"Beg pardon?" Shakespeare said, his mind as sluggish as his body.

"I heard your wife and the girl say they lost rifles. I need your address so I can reimburse you for the loss. My poke is on the other side. My wife never lets it out of her sight."

Blue Water Woman commented, "This is very kind and generous of you."

"Generous nothing," the ferryman said. "I don't want to end up in court like Weston. He operates a ferry half a mile lower down. Not long ago he was taking a herd of cattle across when they spooked and went over the side. Thirty head drowned. The owner took Weston to court and the judge made him pay. So I'm not being generous, lady. I just don't want to be sued."

"We don't know where we will be staying yet," Shakespeare said. "How about if we pick up the money on our way west?"

"It's yours anytime you want it." The ferryman shook and bustled onto the ferry to help unload.

Accepting the mare's reins from his wife, Shakespeare turned to mount.

"I say there! May I have a moment?" asked a small man in a suit in need of an ironing, and a bowler. "One of the other passengers was telling me about your narrow escape. I'd like to hear all about it." He had a pencil and pad. "I'm a reporter for the *Kansas Sun*. Clarence Potts."

"I'd rather not talk about it." Shakespeare lifted his leg to slide his moccasin into the stirrup.

"But it would be a great story," Potts said.

Some people, Shakespeare reflected, just couldn't take hints. "Go find the lady who brought a crate of chickens across. I hear they got seasick."

Evelyn, though, was bubbling with excitement. "Oh, my uncle was wonderful! My aunt can't swim, and he dived right in after her when she was knocked in by those horses!"

"Tell me more," the journalist coaxed, and jotted down the details. His interest heightened when Evelyn mentioned why they had come to Kansas. "You're the younger sister of Zach King? He's been front-page news for weeks! And you'll be too, little darling. Suppose you tell me your full name?"

"Suppose she doesn't," Shakespeare said, and pulled Evelyn away. "Mount up, Ophelia. More of your conversation would infect my brain." He poked Clarence Potts in the chest. "And I'll thank you not to be so familiar with a girl her age."

"Hey, old man, I didn't mean any harm."

Shakespeare balled his right fist, then remembered the incident at the landing, and how the last man he knocked senseless was one of those who had pulled him from the river. He relaxed his fingers and settled for saying, "Call me that again and I'll shove that notebook where you won't get to

write in it until after your next visit to the outhouse."

"Harrumphhh," was the reporter's indignant re-
joinder, and off he went.

Evelyn's lower lip was sticking out. "You can be
cranky at times, Uncle Shakespeare, do you know
that?"

"At times?" Blue Water Woman echoed, and
smiled.

"Females!" Shakespeare climbed onto the mare
and reined toward town. He was trying to be light-
hearted, but he could not stop thinking about the
mishap and the horror of his decision. "Let's find a
place to stay. I'm soaked to the skin and I need to
clean and reload my guns."

"A hot bath might improve your disposition,"
Blue Water Woman remarked.

"O curse of marriage," Shakespeare quoted,
"that we can call these delicate creatures ours, and
not their appetites! I had rather be a toad, and live
upon the vapor of a dungeon, than keep a corner
in the thing I love."

"My, my," Blue Water Woman jousted. "Aren't
we in a mood?"

"My pa gets grumpy too," Evelyn said. "My ma
says it has something to do with men being men."

"You are all in all in spleen," Shakespeare
quoted, "and nothing of a man."

"Isn't he cute when he talks like that?" Evelyn
asked Blue Water Woman.

"That is one word for it."

"I were better to be eaten to death with a rust

than to be scoured to nothing with perpetual jabbering," Shakespeare paraphrased.

Blue Water Woman grinned. "Oh. That was a good one. I cannot tell you what a delight it is to be married to a walking book."

Evelyn thought that was uproariously funny.

As for Shakespeare, he was grateful little else was said until they reached the outskirts of town. Its size amazed him. Five years ago there had been a few cabins and shacks. Now the population had to be upwards of five to six hundred. Streets had been laid out, and building after building constructed. There was a stable and restaurants and a laundry and the newspaper and taverns and saloons and not one but two hotels. Over a square mile of land was encompassed. That included all the outlying houses, cabins, shacks and hovels. The streets were rivers of dust at the moment, but in heavy rain must turn into rivers of mud. Gullies broke the terrain at frequent intervals.

If emigrants continued to flock west, in a few years Kansas would qualify as a full-fledged city.

"So where do you want to stay?" Blue Water Woman ended his contemplation of their surroundings.

After the arduous trial of crossing the plains, after weeks and weeks of sleeping on the hard ground and having to make do with the scantiest of fare, Shakespeare had a hankering to sleep in a soft bed and eat like a glutton. He said as much, ending with, "I say we stay at the best hotel they have."

"Shouldn't we look for Zach first?" Evelyn had been twisting and turning in her saddle as if she expected to come upon her brother any second.

"We're tired and wet and hungry, and our horses are about worn to a frazzle," Shakespeare said. "We take care of them, then we take care of us, then we go find Zach and Louisa."

The stable was full, but the stable owner let them put their horses in the corral out back and promised to see that the animals were fed and watered. He also let them keep their saddles in the tack room for ten cents extra.

A parfleche over each shoulder, Shakespeare paid him. "I saw two hotels on our way in. Which would you say is the best?"

"The Armistead," the man said without hesitation. "They've got a dram shop that sells the finest liquors. And a necessary on every floor, if you can believe that."

"What's a necessary?" Evelyn wanted to know.

"Never you mind." Shakespeare started to leave, but she grabbed his hand and tugged.

"Ask him. Please."

The man overheard. "Ask me what, little one?"

"We're looking for her brother," Shakespeare said. "Maybe you know where we can find him. Zach King?"

Like dew evaporating under a blazing sun, the man's smile evaporated. "I wish I'd known that."

"Is something wrong?"

"No," the man said guardedly. "But I wouldn't

go around telling everyone she's related, were I you."

"Why not?" Evelyn asked.

"Sorry to break it to you, missy, but your brother isn't the most popular person hereabouts right about now. Truth is, if I stood him on a barrel and offered a free shot to everyone who wanted one, half the town would line up."

"That's mean."

"Come along, Evelyn," Blue Water Woman said.

They made off down the street. The comments troubled Shakespeare but not overly so. Soon they would find Zach and Lou, and in a day or two they would be bound for home. Then all would be well.

He couldn't wait.

Chapter Eight

From the restaurant, Largo went straight to The Armistead. He went around to the back and slipped up the stairs when the desk clerk was distracted and climbed to the third floor. He used his key to enter 303 and set the valise on the table. "The lawyer has been disposed of, mistress."

Athena Borke wore a black pelisse that clung to her figure, accenting her many charms. She was sipping a Citronella Jam while seated at a window overlooking the town. "Wainwright did as I instructed him?"

"So he assured me."

"Then go next door," Athena instructed. "And remember. I want them alive."

Largo turned, then immediately turned back again. "With your indulgence, mistress. I am puzzled."

"Be specific," Athena said.

"This elaborate charade we have conducted. Why not dispose of them and be done with it? Why the hundred dollars? Why have Wainwright take a room for them?"

Athena sipped her Citronella Jam. "Where is the pleasure in killing them outright? The breed must suffer as I have suffered. The breed must feel the pain I have felt. Sending you to garrote them would be much too swift and much too elegant."

"But why here? Why do we not take them at the girl's apartment?"

"When would we do it? In the dead of night when their door is bolted and locked? Or in broad daylight, when the street is filled with passersby?"

"I could sneak up the stairs—" Largo began, but his mistress held up a hand.

"And risk being seen? No, I have gone to extraordinary lengths to dispose of any and all who can incriminate us." Athena gazed toward the distant river. "Besides, you must not take the young half-breed lightly. He is a savage, that one. He has lived among the red heathens and been tutored in their barbaric ways. His senses, his reflexes, are sharper than those of normal men."

Largo's cheeks pinched inward. "I am not without skill, mistress."

"Who knows that better than I? But why take unnecessary chances?" Athena took another sip. "Think of this as a game of chess, faithful one. We must plan out all our moves well in advance so when we put the Kings in check, they will be helpless."

Largo still wasn't satisfied. "All our effort to cover our tracks, yet we take a suite next to theirs?"

"For two reasons. First, I refuse to stay at The Missourian. As a hotel it would make an excellent pig pen. The Armistead is the only place worthy of my patronage, and even here they barely meet my standards."

"And the second reason, mistress?"

"Convenience. We will take them out the back in the early hours before dawn. No one will wonder at their absence. It will be assumed they returned to the Rockies, and good riddance." Athena smiled. "Is anything else troubling you?"

"As always I am in awe of your brilliance." Largo bowed. "I will go do as you bid me."

The suite in 304 was nearly identical to 303; the same spacious rooms, the same rich red carpet, the same dark brown walls, the same two bedrooms, the same large closets. The one noticeable difference was a cart by the front door. On it sat a silver tray, and on the tray stood a bottle of wine with a card attached: *Courtesy of the management.*

From his jacket pocket Largo removed a corkscrew he brought specifically for the purpose of opening the complimentary bottle. He did so with the utmost care, and when the cork was out, he dipped his huge fingers into a different pocket and palmed a vial that he treated as gingerly as he would the most fragile glass. It, too, was capped by a cork, which he carefully removed. Then, being sure not to spill the contents, he poured about a thimbleful of white powder from the vial into the wine bottle.

Largo slowly swirled the wine so the powder became thoroughly mixed. Then he corked the vial and slid it into his pocket. He sealed the wine bottle with a new cork and set it in the middle of the silver tray.

Now came the part Largo was not looking forward to, because it meant he must be separated from his mistress. He walked to the second bedroom, opened the closet, backed into it, and slid the door shut. Squatting, he folded his enormous arms across his knees and settled down to wait for as long as was necessary.

Eventually the Kings would come.

And be undone.

"No," Zach said for the tenth time in half an hour. "Why do you keep asking me when my answer is always the same?"

"Because I want to go," Louisa said. "Just think. A night at the best hotel to be found between here and St. Louis. And for free!" She stepped to the window. "It will be dark soon. Please."

"It's enough that we're keeping the hundred dollars. We'll probably wake up tomorrow and find out charges have been filed against us for stealing it."

"You can be such a worrywart, do you know that?" Lou said. "What's your real reason?"

Zach glanced up in mild exasperation from the sofa. "When did you turn into a nag?"

"And when did you start insulting me?" Lou stalked to the door. "I can see this will get me nowhere. I need some fresh air."

"I'll go with you."

"No. You lie there and try to remember what it was like to be a human being. I haven't often asked much of you, Zach King. The one time I do, you act like we're walking into a Blackfoot ambush." Lou had one parting shot left. "Believe it or not, there are nice people in this world. People who do generous things for others because they think it's right."

Lou slammed the door. It was childish, but she was mad. After all she had gone through on his behalf, after all the uncertainty and anguish, he wouldn't indulge one little request. Men could be so pigheaded!

A brisk breeze was blowing. Lou broke out in goosebumps and almost went back up to fetch her shawl. Instead, she wrapped her arms tight about her and started walking. She didn't care where she went, just so she stayed in motion. She was too agitated to stand still.

A variety of scents tingled Lou's nose; the dust of the street, the horse droppings that littered the ground like obscenely bloated flapjacks, fragrant hints of food on the stove. Snatches of conversation drifted in and out of her hearing. She passed countless pedestrians without seeing them.

Suddenly Lou stopped. A new scent made her realize how far she had come; the smell of water. She had reached the west edge of town and saw the river glistening in the twilight like a broad serpent.

Wheeling, Lou took several steps—and stopped again. Twenty yards away a figure had darted between buildings to keep from being seen. A tall figure in a brown hat and a brown jacket. She realized it was the man who had been following them earlier. And now he was following her!

The street was practically deserted. The supper hour was a quiet hour when hardly anyone was abroad. She was on her own, and she had left all her weapons at the apartment. Turning left, she crossed an unfenced yard to the next street and turned again, heading back into town. She expected the man to follow her and was taken aback when he appeared at the corner of a building up ahead. He had cut across a yard to cut her off.

Lou fought down bubbling panic. She was a King, by damn. She had fought hostiles, had survived blizzards and bears and mountain lions. She would rely on her wits and the skills her husband

and father-in-law and mother-in-law had taught her. She ran north, past a cabin and an outhouse from which the most abominable reek issued. Her aim was to elude her stalker, then swing east again to the apartment. She was a swift runner. Everyone said so. For a hundred yards she ran at her top speed. Then, darting behind a shack, she peeked out.

The man in brown was nowhere in sight.

Lou thought she had succeeded. But seconds later he strode into view, glancing this way and that. Clearly, he had lost track of her but knew she was somewhere near and was determined to find her. His jacket was open, and she could see the pepperbox. Suddenly he looked toward the shack and Lou ducked back. Breathless, she waited half a minute, then peeked out.

The man was gone.

Emboldened, Lou continued north, crossing yard after yard. She was almost to a ramshackle house when a dog on a rope came rushing out of nowhere and barked furiously, raising enough racket to be heard in St. Louis. Avoiding it, she ran on.

That was when the back door to the house opened and a grungy man in a greasy shirt came out. "Hey! What are you doin' skulkin' around my place, boy?"

What with her short hair and loose-fitting buckskins, Lou was often mistaken for a male. Zach had made the same mistake when they first met. She kept on going without answering.

"Didn't you hear me?" the grungy man bellowed. "Are you a thief, lookin' to steal something?"

Resentment sparked Lou to respond, "I'm no thief! I'm just out for a stroll."

"Sure you are. And I'm the president and this here is the White House."

Lou ignored greasy shirt, thinking he would stop pestering her and go back inside. But he started after her at a jog.

"Stop, I say!" he bellowed. "We've had a rash of thievery around here, and I bet you're the culprit!"

"Jackass!" Lou said without thinking.

The man's cheeks puffed out in anger and he came on faster. "I'll get the truth out of you, boy, one way or another!"

This was the last thing Lou needed. She ran flat-out, across a weed-strewn yard to a street. She had doubled the gap, but he was still doggedly in pursuit. Swearing under her breath, she hoped he tripped and broke his fool leg.

Then another man came out of a house and said something to greasy shirt, and whatever greasy shirt replied caused the second man to give chase, too.

Lou flew on. Only a few more houses and cabins to go and she would be at the north edge of town. A tract of woodland promised sanctuary and she bounded for it like an antelope fleeing wolves. When next she glanced back, she couldn't believe her eyes; four men were now after her. They must all think she was the thief.

Stopping to explain, Lou realized, was pointless.

They would think she made up the story of the man in brown. Better for her to lose them in the woods and go her own way.

Fate chose that moment to play a hand. A rough-hewn woman in a plain dress came out of the last cabin and began shaking out a blanket.

"Stop that one!" greasy shirt shouted. "He's a thief!"

Lou angled to the left to give the cabin a wider berth, but the woman had dropped the blanket and was moving to intercept her. "I am not a thief!" she cried, to no effect.

"Hold on there, boy!" the woman said, moving faster. "Do the right thing and give yourself up."

Lou pumped her legs with renewed vigor. The woman lunged, a hand clawing at her buckskins, but Lou swerved and made it past and then all she had to cross was a short field and she would be in among the trees, and safe.

A growl proved her wrong.

Lou glanced back. Someone had unleashed a mongrel. Its neck hairs bristling, its teeth bared, it was rapidly overtaking her.

What had started as comical had turned deadly serious. Lou had no hope of reaching the woods before the dog reached her. She spied several rocks, and bending, snatched one up in either hand, then ran on.

Lou's timing had to be perfect. She glanced back, marking the distance between them, and when the dog was ten feet away she stopped and whirled and threw the rock in her right hand. It caught the dog full in the face and the dog yelped and veered. Her second rock caught it in the front legs and the dog reversed direction.

Lou had always been good at chucking rocks. When she was a kid, she practiced by the hour until she could hit anything she set her mind to.

Soon Lou came to the trees. She hoped her pursuers had finally given up. But no, only one had stopped and was tending to the dog while the rest, including the woman, were still after her.

Let them come, Lou thought. In the woods she was in her element. They would never catch her now. She zigzagged into the undergrowth and after twenty yards turned east.

Suddenly the vegetation ended at the brink of a steep gully. On the other side the woods resumed.

Lou descended in long hops. Midway down the slope was loose dirt, and as her left heel came down, her leg shot out from under her and she fell end over end like a wind-blown tumbleweed. She hit the bottom hard. Pain spiked her ribs and the breath whooshed from her lungs.

Loud voices spurred Lou into sitting up. She got to her hands and knees and began crawling up the opposite slope. Once at the top she would lie low until her pursuers gave up.

"Here he is!"

Boots thudded behind her. Lou tried to stand, to run, but rough hands seized her and she was hauled to her feet and shaken as a terrier might shake a rat.

"I've got him! This way!"

"Let me go!" Lou protested, struggling. She was thrown to the ground on her stomach and a foot was pressed against her back, pinning her.

"You're not going anywhere, thief. We're about to make an example of you no one will ever forget."

"I haven't done anything!"

It was greasy shirt. He bent and slapped her and laughed. "That's what they always say."

Over the side of the gully came the rest, the other men and the woman, their faces slick with sweat and twisted with hate.

"Say your prayers, boy," greasy shirt said. "Your string has played out."

Chapter Nine

Shakespeare McNair could count the number of times he had stayed at a hotel on one hand. He was seventeen when he left civilization for the untamed vastness of the remote Rockies and had rarely been back since. The wilderness intoxicated him. Life was a daily delight of exploration and discovery. He fell in love with the land as well as the people and never entertained a desire to leave. From time to time he did, of course, but only to obtain supplies or buy a new rifle or have a broken pistol fixed. On those occasions he usually shunned habitations and slept out under the stars.

The few occasions Shakespeare stayed at hotels had all been in St. Louis at the same establishment, a small, rustic place that catered to frontiersmen. The Wilton, it was called, after its owner, a former mountain man.

It could not begin to compare to The Armistead.

For starters, there was the carpet. Shakespeare took four steps and stopped in bewilderment, unaccustomed to walking on a sponge. "Danged if this don't beat all," he said while raising and lowering his right foot a few times.

"You've never walked on carpet before?" Evelyn asked.

"Not carpet as thick as three or four bearskin rugs, no," Shakespeare said. He looked forward to getting a room and taking off his moccasins so he could wriggle his toes in it.

"My folks took me to a hotel in New Orleans once that had carpet like this," Evelyn said. "They serve food right in your room, and clean your clothes if you ask them." Her eyes were aglitter with rapture. "And you wonder why I want to live in a city."

"We'll miss you, is all," Shakespeare said. More than she would ever know.

A light tinkling from overhead drew Shakespeare's gaze to a crystal chandelier that glittered like a hundred sparkling diamonds. The effect was mesmerizing. He stood gaping until his wife plucked at his sleeve.

"We can catch flies later. Right now Evelyn and I

need hot baths before she comes down with a cold."

"First things first." Shakespeare marched to the front desk and plopped his parfleches down.

"Welcome to The Armistead, sir." A clerk in a natty suit bestowed an amused smile. "On behalf of the management, permit me to say that our staff is devoted to making your stay as enjoyable as possible. If there is anything you want, anything at all, all you need do is ask."

"A room would be nice," Shakespeare said.

"Two beds? I presume your daughter will be sleeping with your wife?"

Shakespeare and Evelyn chortled. "I should be so lucky as to have her as my own." He was about to mention that she was the product of Nate and Winona King's passion when he remembered the stable owner's admonition. "Do you have a room with three beds?"

"Only our luxury suites on the top floor," the clerk said. He hesitated, then added, "And they are quite expensive."

Shakespeare touched his possibles bag. "Boldness comes to me now," he quoted, "and brings me heart." He took out his poke. "What do you call expensive in these parts, pardner?"

"Ten dollars a night. That includes a complimentary bottle of wine."

"Why, as all comforts are, most good, most good indeed," Shakespeare said. But he was thinking that ten dollars was more than most people earned in a month when he was Evelyn's age. He turned to Blue Water Woman. "What do you say, my love?"

"It would be a new experience."

"A costly one."

"Only for a skinflint." Blue Water Woman could more than hold her own. "What else do we spend our money on?"

The truth of the matter was that Shakespeare had seven thousand dollars socked away in a cubby hole under their cabin. Most was acquired during his trapping years, when a good season's take could reap close to two thousand dollars. He had brought three hundred along for spending money. An extravagance, since on their last several visits east he barely spent fifty.

"A suite it is, then, by thunder," Shakespeare said, and thumped the desk for emphasis.

"You'll need to sign in," the clerk said, turning the register. "An X will suffice if you can't write."

For a few seconds Shakespeare was speechless. "Oh, ye giddy goose."

"Sir?"

"I will throw thee from my care forever into the staggers and the careless lapse of youth and ignorance."

"Sir?"

Shakespeare took up the quill pen with a flourish. "I will have you know, sir, that I am on most intimate terms with the Bard. I have perused Plato, that master of questions within questions, and set sail with brave Odysseus on seas of terror. I have feasted my eye on Herodotus, and reveled in the immortal courage of the indomitable Leonidas. What say you to that?"

The clerk looked in confusion to Blue Water Woman.

"That is his way of telling you he can write. My husband never uses one word when fifty will do."

"Oh."

Shakespeare had started to sign in the appropriate space, but stopped. "Don't listen to her. She is too mean to have her name repeated."

"She seems awful nice to me, sir," the clerk said.

"Only because you aren't married to the wench. Her insolence, sir, makes Circe appear timid, the Cyclops appear tame." Out of pique, Shakespeare took up two lines so his signature was twice as large as all the rest. "There. Feast your eyes on excellence."

"Well done, sir. And might I say, I have never met anyone quite like you."

"He quotes William Shakespeare by the minute," Blue Water Woman explained. "I have heard them so often, I know a few quotes myself." She paused. "Let me see. What is that one I am thinking of? Oh yes." Her smile was deviltry personified. "He speaks nothing but madman."

Shakespeare puffed out his cheeks in mock indignation. "Of all the bard's magnificent pearls, leave it to you to remember that one." He reached for the parfleches and discovered a boy in a red jacket had one under each arm. "Hold. What villainy is this?"

"He's the bellboy, sir," the clerk said. "He will carry your things up for you and help you settle in."

"I am perfectly capable of carrying my own things," Shakespeare said. "I still have all my teeth and my head has not so much ear wax as brains."

"Husband," Blue Water Woman said.

"Oh, all right. But I swear. If anyone offers to undress me, I'll gut them like a fish and use their innards for rope."

"Bluster," Blue Water Woman said to the clerk and bellboy. "He is the gentlest of souls and kindest of men."

"Lead on," Shakespeare gruffly declared. "After this verbal assault my ears are blistered and my head is reeling."

Bronze rails bordered the stairs. On each landing was a silver spittoon. Paintings adorned the walls, including one of a fox hunt in England that fascinated Evelyn.

At the third landing they met a woman coming down. She was tall and dressed all in black and had lustrous black hair that cascaded past her shoulders. She nodded at them and swished on by.

"Goodness gracious, she was beautiful," Evelyn breathed in awe.

"And rich," the bellboy commented. "She has her own carriage and her own manservant to wait on her hand and foot. Why, when she arrived, she had more luggage than ten of most of our usual guests."

"Wealth isn't everything," Shakespeare said.

"It sure beats being poor," was the bellboy's assessment. "Word is, she married into a wealthy Eastern family. Her husband died a few years ago and she inherited everything. But she never uses his name, which is strange."

"I would love to have a rich husband," Evelyn said.

Blue Water Woman had one more arrow in her quiver. "I would be happy to have a sane one."

The bellboy announced, "Here we are. Three-oh-five." He inserted a key and held the door so they might precede him. "There are two bedrooms, each with its own wash basin. The necessary is at the end of the hall to the left."

Evelyn's interest perked. "There's that word again."

"Your complimentary wine will be brought up shortly. The maid changes the linen each morning and brings fresh towels. Should you not want to be disturbed, hang out the sign on the door. For room service, you pull the cord, here, and it will ring a bell below."

"Do you tuck us in at night?" Shakespeare asked.

The bellboy wasn't finished. "The hallway lamps are lit as soon as the sun goes down and stay lit until midnight. At one A.M. the front doors and back doors are locked and stay locked until four A.M. A desk clerk, though, is on duty twenty-four hours a day."

"This place would be perfect if it had stalls for horses," Shakespeare said, and reached for the parfleches.

"Will there be anything else, sir?"

"No, you can go." Shakespeare moved to the

door to close it but the bellboy just stood there, waiting expectantly. "What? Do you want me to read to you?"

"No, sir," the bellboy said, and coughed.

"You're supposed to give him what my pa calls a gratuity," Evelyn remarked. "For being so helpful."

"Had I known you were a leech I'd have carried my own parfleches," Shakespeare grumbled. He gave the boy a dollar.

"I thank you, sir. You are a true gentleman."

"What else would I be?" Shakespeare rejoined, and resisted an impulse to kick the imp on his way out. He carried their parfleches into the first bedroom and set them on the bed, which was twice the size of their own and softer than a fawn's backside. He stretched out on his back and closed his eyes.

"Husband, Evelyn and I are taking baths. The bellboy told her they will fill a tub for us and provide a bar of lye soap."

"Have fun. I don't need a bath right now."

"Yes, you do."

Shakespeare cracked his right eye open. "Are you implying I'm a mite ripe?"

"Only when I breathe next to you," Blue Water Woman said. "Come along and we will take turns. Evelyn will use the tub first, then me, then you."

"If I smell the worst, why do I get the dirtiest water?"

"You are the man."

"I do not strain at the position. It is familiar."

"Come then," Blue Water Woman coaxed. "Evelyn and I want to feel clean again, and to use our noses."

Shakespeare rolled his eyes at the ceiling. "I am an ass, indeed. You may prove it by my long ears."

Athena Borke sat in the lobby for three hours in a high-backed chair in a secluded corner where the shadows hid her from those who entered. After the first hour her perfect features were marred by a frown that grew as time passed. Her left shoe continually tapped the floor. Her fingernails tapped the chair arm.

Finally Athena could not bear the wait any longer and rose to go to her suite. She saw a lad with an armload of newspapers enter and hand a dozen to the desk clerk, who paid him with a shiny new coin.

"Any news worth reading today, Bobby?"

"Not much, Mr. Timms. A man's heart gave out and he died with his face in a bowl of soup. A hog was run over by a buckboard and the buckboard tipped over and the driver broke his leg. And the mayor is upset at all the animal droppings in the streets. He says it will give the town a bad name so he wants to outlaw all pigs, chickens, dogs, cats and cows."

"Too bad we can't outlaw the mayor."

"Oh. And some people nearly drowned in the Missouri this morning when a horse went wild on a ferry and they were knocked off."

"No shootings, knifings or beatings?" The desk

clerk was disappointed. "You're right. Not much interesting."

By then Athena was at the foot of the stairs.

"One thing has folks talking," Bobby said. "One of those people who fell in the river is the sister of that guy everyone wants hung. You know, the renegade who killed those traders and was put on trial."

"Zach King?"

"That's him. Well, I have to scoot. Mr. Barnes will throw a fit if I don't get all these delivered fast enough." The boy hastened out.

Crossing to the desk, Athena picked up a copy. "Do you mind if I take one of these?"

"Not at all, Miss Borke. The *Kansas Sun* is free to guests."

Simmering with excitement, Athena could barely restrain herself until she reached her suite. The edition was six pages, half of them advertisements. On the second to last page she found the story she was looking for and devoured it, then read the account again.

"It doesn't mention their names," Athena said aloud. She smiled a smile that would chill anyone who saw it. "But that can be remedied."

Athena pulled the cord for the bellboy. At his timid knock she called out for him to enter, stated the errand she wanted him to run, and gave him five dollars as incentive.

"I'm more than happy to help, ma'am, but Timms at the front desk won't like me being gone as long as this might take."

"Tell him it's for me."

"Yes, ma'am, but it's against the rules for bellboys to leave the hotel. And Timms isn't one to go against the owner's wishes."

"Do you suppose five dollars for him would smooth things over?"

"Oh, yes, ma'am. He loves money as much as I do."

"Don't we all?" Athena Borke said.

Chapter Ten

Louisa King was hauled to her feet. She tried to break free but there were too many. She was pushed. She was slapped. She was punched. The man with the greasy shirt, the one who had started it all, shook her again. Shook her so hard, her teeth rattled.

"You're the thief who's been stealin' my tools, aren't you, boy? Sneakin' right into my house and takin' 'em right out from under my nose?"

"No, no," Lou said, but he didn't believe her.

"Bet you weren't figurin' on me borrowin' my brother's dog to guard my house, were you?" greasy shirt boasted. "It was his barkin' that gave you away."

"I've never stolen anything!"

"Sure you haven't!" said another man. "I've had things taken, too. A watch my mother gave me. A folding knife I had since I was a kid."

"It wasn't me!" Lou tried again. "I've only been in town a short while."

"You must take us for fools," said someone else.

The woman in the plain dress jabbed Lou in the shoulder. "I guess you never heard 'Thou Shalt Not Steal.'"

"What should we do?" a man asked. "Tar and feather him and run him out of Kansas on a rail?"

"I ain't got any tar," greasy shirt said, "and findin' a rail would take too long." He smirked. "I've got a better idea. I say we beat him with switches until he's so black and blue, he'll think twice before he ever steals again."

"I like that idea," said the woman.

A man turned to climb up the gully. "I'll go find the switches. There must be plenty of branches lying about." He took a step, then stopped. "Say. Who's that?"

All eyes rose to the top. Lou looked, too, and her plight went from bad to worse. The man in the brown hat had found her. "What do you think you're doing?" he demanded.

"This here boy is a thief," greasy shirt said. "We're about to make an example of him."

"Let go of her," the man in brown commanded.

"Her?" Greasy shirt and the others glanced at Lou. "Are you telling us this here is a girl?"

"Her name is Louisa King. Whatever you are accusing her of, you're mistaken. Release her and go about your business."

One of the other men was skeptical. "Wait a minute. How is it you know so much about her?

How do we know the two of you aren't in cahoots? Who the hell are you, anyhow?"

Lou was as surprised as her captors by the answer.

"I'm Major Dan Bannister from Fort Leavenworth."

"So you claim," greasy shirt said. "But where's your uniform? What proof do you have that you are who you say?"

The man in brown opened his jacket and placed his hand on the pepperbox. "I'm not about to bandy words. You will release her, and you will release her this minute, or by the Eternal you will wish you had."

Bannister's tone, to say nothing of the threat, convinced the vigilantes to back off, but they weren't happy about being deprived of their prey.

"I'm going to the fort tomorrow," greasy shirt said. "I'll talk to whoever is in charge and find out if you lied."

"Go right ahead," Bannister said, descending the slope with lithe ease, his back ramrod straight. "Ask for Colonel Templeton, my superior. He also happens to be the post commander."

The woman was more observant than her companions. "Maybe this gentleman really is in the army. He sure carries himself like a soldier."

"Be off with you," Major Bannister ordered, and when they strayed toward town, he turned. "Are you all right, Mrs. King? Did they hurt you?"

"No," Lou mumbled. She shook off her confusion and smoothed her buckskin shirt. "I don't understand, Major. Why have you been following my husband and me? What's this all about?"

Major Bannister studied the thick woods rimming the gully. "I suggest we talk somewhere else. We're too vulnerable here." He took her arm and ushered her up the slope and off through the trees, his other hand never straying from the pepperbox.

"You act as if someone is out to get us," Lou commented.

"Not us, Mrs. King. You and your husband." A sound caused Bannister to whirl but it was only a gray squirrel scampering among the branches. "I have reason to suspect the two of you are in grave danger."

The officer did not say more until they had reached town. The were hurrying along a dusty street and came to a butcher shop. The shop was closed, but there was a bench in front where customers could wait while their orders were filled.

"This will do."

"I'm listening," Lou said as she sat. "Don't keep me in suspense."

The major was gazing up and down the street. "There's no sign of him so I guess we're safe enough for the moment." He sank down, as tense and wary as a panther.

"No sign of whom?"

Bannister faced her. "I should start at the beginning, with Colonel Templeton."

"A fine man," Lou said. The colonel was the only person who treated Zach decently after his arrest.

One of the few who hadn't leaped to judgment, and didn't have a bigoted bone in his body.

"None finer," Major Bannister agreed. "He assigned me to keep an eye on the two of you, and to snoop around and find out what else I could."

"You've just begun and already you make no sense."

"I'm sorry, Mrs. King," Bannister apologized. "It's been nerve-wracking, always having to watch over my shoulder. Never knowing when I might end up like the rest. I haven't slept more than two hours a night. I'm tired and worn out and it's made me careless."

"I'm still at a loss."

Bannister leaned on one hand. "What do you know about the Borke brothers?"

"The pair my husband killed? Artemis set up a trading post in the Green River country and tried to start a war between the Shoshones and the Crows so he could line his pockets selling rifles to both. He also sold whiskey, which added to the trouble." Lou rubbed her arms where greasy shirt had squeezed her. "Phineas came west wanting revenge. He kidnapped me and tried to lure my husband into an ambush, but Zach turned the tables."

"Did you know they had a sister?"

Lou nodded. "So someone mentioned. She never showed up at the trial, though."

"Wrong. She was there the whole time. She always sat in the back of the courtroom and never told anyone who she was. Anyone, that is, except Colonel Templeton when she visited the fort."

"When was this?"

"Right after your husband was brought in. She arrived in town about a week before Phineas left for the mountains, rented a house under an assumed name, and laid low until word came that Phineas had been killed and your husband was in custody. Then she came to see Colonel Templeton and demanded to know what the army was going to do. When the colonel told her it hadn't been decided yet, she pressured him to have your husband turned over to the civilian authorities to stand trail. In the interests of fairness and justice, she said."

"Strange. You would think she'd want my husband up before a firing squad. Nearly everyone else does."

"Colonel Templeton thought it odd, as well. Even more so when he had me do some checking and I found out about her assumed name and where she was staying. Athena Borke is a wealthy woman but she and that servant of hers were staying in a dump."

"Athena? That's a pretty name." Lou sobered. "She's so rich she has servants?"

"Just one. From what I understand, he travels with her everywhere she goes. His name is Largo. Twice I've seen him watching your apartment." Bannister scanned the street once more. "Colonel Templeton asked me to keep an eye on you and your husband so that you don't come to harm."

"And here we thought you were out to hurt us." Lou laughed in relief.

"The colonel and I believe Athena Borke wants

revenge for her brothers and will stop at nothing to get it."

"Just because she had her servant spy on us?"

"Hardly. The day before last the house she was renting burned down. Five bodies were found in the rubble. So far two have been identified as the jury foreman and one of the jurors who set your husband free. It looks like the other bodies are more missing jurors."

"Oh my," Lou said.

"There's more. A lawyer I saw her servant speaking to died under mysterious circumstances."

"You're saying she's killed six people?"

"Or Largo has. Colonel Templeton thought it time to warn you, which is why I followed you when you left your apartment. Stay on your guard, Mrs. King. Be on the lookout for anything out of the ordinary. Above all, be extremely suspicious of strangers."

Lou suddenly straightened. "Wait a second. Did you say something about a lawyer?"

"Mortimer Wainwright. A rather shady fellow. He didn't have the highest of reputations. He was eating at a restaurant when he keeled over. The cause of death has yet to be ascertained."

"My God," Lou breathed.

"What's wrong? You look as if you're ill."

In a rush Lou told him about Wainwright's visit, about the hundred dollars, about the suite at The Armistead reserved by a mysterious benefactor. She even told him about her argument with Zach.

Major Bannister listened with rising interest. "I

warrant your husband is right. Whatever Athena Borke is up to, it doesn't bode well. Stay away from The Armistead. You go there at your peril."

"Surely she wouldn't try anything in a hotel full of people?" Lou said, her dream of spending the night in luxury fading like a will-o'-the-wisp.

"I wouldn't put anything past her," the major said. "If she's anything like her brothers, she has no scruples whatsoever."

"Why hasn't she been arrested?"

A noise from down the street brought Major Bannister to his feet, but it was only a couple of pigs rooting around. One had bumped over a small barrel. Bannister relaxed and said, "The marshal can't arrest anyone without proof, and Athena Borke had been most meticulous about covering her tracks."

"Doesn't the marshal know about her connection to the jurors and Wainwright?"

"*Possible* connection," the officer stressed. "And no. I haven't told him."

Lou was flabbergasted. "Why not? What are you waiting for? My husband to be measured for a pine box?"

"I can't go to Marshal Owen with wild accusations against a woman as rich and powerful as this Borke woman. I don't have enough to put her behind bars. All the marshal could do is question her."

"At least she would know we were on to her."

"Is that wise? Forewarning her would make her doubly careful."

"Maybe she would give up and go home."

"I very much doubt that anything will stop her from carrying out her vendetta," Major Bannister said. "I've done some checking, and she isn't the kind to quit once she sets her mind to something."

"Where is this Borke woman now?" Lou was not about to twiddle her thumbs while the shrew played cat and mouse with her husband. If she had learned anything from her in-laws, it was that frontiersmen—and frontier women—dealt with trouble head-on.

Major Bannister looked embarrassed. "I'm sorry to say, I don't know. I assume she rented another house, but I haven't had time to locate where. Except when reporting to the colonel, I spend every waking minute keeping an eye on you and your husband." He grew thoughtful. "You know, though—" he said, and stopped.

"What?"

"Nothing. I couldn't possibly ask it."

"Ask what?" Lou pressed him.

"This room at The Armistead," Major Bannister said. "If we're right, Athena must be behind it. Maybe she intends to have her servant slit your throats in the middle of the night."

"I'd like to see him try. My husband is the lightest sleeper on the planet. He wakes up at the drop of a feather."

"You're missing my point," Bannister said. "We can use this to our advantage and catch them in the act."

"Set ourselves up as bait? That's a great idea."

"It's a dangerous idea that could get you and your husband killed."

"Not him. He refuses to go." Lou stood up. She had made up her mind. She would save Zach herself. "I'll be the bait."

"No."

"Why not? Borke is out to kill my husband, isn't she? It's fitting I handle this woman-to-woman."

"You're forgetting her servant, Largo."

"That's where you come in. You deal with him, I deal with her, and we end this." Lou started briskly off toward the center of town, but Bannister caught up and caught hold of her arm.

"Please, Mrs. King. I beg you. Think this through."

"I already have."

"You're being extremely rash and foolhardy."

Lou faced him. "It would be more foolish to do nothing. The room at The Armistead is our best hope of stopping her. You can come along if you want, or you can go back to the fort and tell Colonel Templeton we thank him kindly, but we don't need your help." She marched on, resolved to see it through.

Muttering something about "women," Major Bannister fell into step beside her.

Chapter Eleven

Evelyn King was in heaven. She loved The Armistead. Its luxury dazzled her: the plush carpet, the shimmering chandelier, the mahogany wood paneling, the way everyone waited on them. She would not mind living there the rest of her life.

Evelyn knew her parents weren't happy about her decision to leave the Rockies one day. They didn't understand why she was so fond of civilization. Or, as her father put it, why she wanted to give up the freedom of the frontier for prison.

She tried to explain. She tried to make them see that for all its flaws, civilization had a lot to offer. An easier life, for one thing. Instead of spending days curing a hide and cutting and sewing to make buckskins, she could buy clothes right off a store shelf. Instead of spending hours toiling over a hot stove or cook pot, she could buy her meals at any place that served hot food.

Then there was the fear factor. To Evelyn it made no sense to live where grizzlies and mountain lions and hostiles posed a constant threat when she could live where the worst thing that could happen would be stubbing her toe on a boardwalk.

Other points, too, Evelyn brought up with her parents, but they were still against the idea.

Her father was deeply hurt. Evelyn saw it in his eyes when the subject came up. He had been born and raised in New York City but loved the wilderness despite its many dangers. "Out here we can live as we please," he once told her. "In New York I couldn't."

Evelyn had been to the States several times and had met scores who came from there. So she replied, "You make it sound like people have no say at all."

"Many don't. Slavery is a common practice. Blacks enslaved to whites. Whites lorded over by politicians. Politicians under the control of the rich and the powerful. No one east of the Mississippi River is truly free."

"There's nothing to stop me from being a teacher if I want and that's freedom enough for me."

Her father had put his hand on her shoulder and led her to a log and sat beside her. "There are other things to consider. Crime is everywhere. Footpads steal everyone blind. Murders are common. Most folks work long hours for little pay and never get ahead."

"Here I can't step out the cabin door without having to watch out for rattlers or bears or worse," Evelyn had brought up. "I can't go for rides without having to worry about the Bloods or the Piegans or the Sioux."

"Nowhere in this world is perfectly safe."

"But some places are more safe than others," Evelyn ended the debate.

Now here she was, enjoying a taste of luxury,

while her father lay back on the trail recuperating from severe wounds inflicted by a black bear. Extra proof, as if any were needed, that the wilderness was a far more perilous—and undesirable—place to live.

Evelyn grinned as she skipped down the stairs to the lobby. Shakespeare and Blue Water Woman were resting before venturing out to find a restaurant, and she had some time to herself. The desk clerk was sorting through letters. Skipping over, she stood with her hands clasped behind her back.

"Yes, young lady?"

"I'm just watching," Evelyn said.

The clerk was a friendly sort. "I've noticed you seem to be enjoying yourself."

"You have no idea. When I grow up I'm going to live in a town just like this one, or bigger."

"By the time you grow up this one will *be* bigger," the clerk said. "In the last month alone, according to the newspaper, eleven new businesses have opened, one of them a dress shop you might find worth a visit."

Evelyn looked down at her plain homespun garment. Her mother always wore a buckskin dress and had hinted more than once how pleased she would be if Evelyn did the same. But Evelyn liked the softer feel of homespun. "My ma made this for me."

"It's quite fetching," the clerk said, "but not nearly as fetching as hers." He was staring toward the stairs.

Descending them was the lovely lady with lustrous black hair. Her black dress had more lace and frills than Evelyn ever saw. Like the clerk, she could not help admiring it.

The lady came over and asked in a low voice that made Evelyn think of the purr of a cat, "Has the bellboy returned yet, Mr. Timms?"

"Not yet, no," the clerk said. "As soon as he does I'll send him to your suite."

"Thank you." The woman glanced down, and smiled. "What have we here? You're quite pretty, child."

"My name is Evelyn."

"I'm Athena. Pleased to make your acquaintance."

"You're pretty yourself," Evelyn said by way of a compliment. She would never admit it, but the lady in black was even more gorgeous than her mother, which took some doing.

"Why, aren't you precious?" Athena said, and squeezed Evelyn's shoulder. "What would you say if I offered to treat you to ice cream in the hotel dining room?"

"What's ice cream?" Evelyn asked.

Both the lady and the clerk laughed, and Athena said, "Where have you been keeping yourself all your life, my dear? On the moon? Ice cream is the food of the gods, a culinary ambrosia unlike any other."

Evelyn loved how the lady talked. "Does it taste good?"

"You can decide for yourself." Taking Evelyn by the hand, Athena crossed to an arched doorway.

The spacious room beyond was ablaze with color—flowers and paintings and brass fixtures.

A man in a white jacket came scurrying to meet them. "Your usual table, madam?"

"Certainly," Athena said.

No sooner were they seated in chairs covered with satin than a younger man came running, a waiter who bowed and placed two menus before them. "Would madam care for her usual glass of wine before ordering?"

"Not this time. And we won't need these." Athena handed the menus back. "My young friend and I would like some ice cream. Chocolate, I should think, unless she prefers some other flavor."

"Chocolate is fine," Evelyn said, amazed at her good fortune. Chocolate was a rare treat back home. In the winter they had hot chocolate sometimes, and on a couple of occasions her mother had treated her to chocolate cake from a recipe her father remembered from his childhood.

"So then," Athena said, folding her slender hands, "tell me all about yourself. Where are you from and what are you doing in this godforsaken mud hole?"

Evelyn gazed around them. "It's cleaner here than any place I've ever been."

"I was referring to Kansas," Athena said. "Compared to New York or Paris or Rome, it's a dung heap."

"You've been to Paris and Rome!" Evelyn exclaimed in pure envy. "What are they like? How long were you there? Did you go to the theater and the opera and concerts?"

"Slow down, little one," Athena said with a chuckle. "You're a bundle of curiosity, aren't you?"

"I've always had a hankering to visit faraway places," Evelyn said. "My uncle tells me that in Paris ladies wear hats as high as trees and in Rome men run around in dresses."

Athena's delicate eyebrows rose half an inch. "I would like to meet this uncle of yours. But the latest Parisian hats are only half as high as trees and Roman men only run around in dresses on special holidays."

Evelyn realized the lady was joking with her, and giggled. "What are they really like?"

"More wonderful than I can describe," Athena said. "In Paris you can stroll along the Seine and in an hour see more fashions than you would in a year anywhere else. In Rome there are so many shops and sights you could spend a lifetime and not visit them all."

"And New York City?"

"The people are always rude, the streets are always crowded, the buildings are built one next to the other. Yet it has an air of exhilaration about it that you will find nowhere else."

"I can't wait to go," Evelyn said. "My father was born there but he never wants to go back."

"And your mother?"

"She's a homebody. She loves our cabin, loves our valley. The only time she leaves is to visit her kin."

"People should never forget their roots," Athena said. "My family was poor when I was your age, but my brothers and I were very close. There wasn't anything we wouldn't do for each other."

"I have a brother," Evelyn said. "We're close too. But we spatted a lot when we were young."

"That's normal. So did my brothers and I." Athena seemed to gaze off into the distance. "I remember one time I pushed them in the pond for pulling my pigtails. Those were the days."

"Brothers can be mean. But they can be nice, too," Evelyn said. "Do you have any sisters? I always wanted one to play dolls with and things."

"No sisters, sorry to say. I would have liked one. Although I hear that sisters fight just as much if not more than brothers and sisters do."

"I don't see how that can be."

Athena glanced toward the lobby. Evelyn did likewise and saw that from where they sat, they could see the entrance. An older gentleman had just come in and was hobbling toward the front desk.

"Do you know him?"

"What? Oh, no," Athena said. "But I am expecting someone anytime now. I hope the waiter hurries up with our ice cream."

Hardly were the words out of her mouth than he reappeared carrying a silver tray. "Here you are, madam." He set a bowl in front of Athena and another in front of Evelyn. Athena began unfolding a cloth napkin that lay in front of her, so Evelyn unfolded hers. Inside was a spoon.

"Look at what I found."

"We can't eat ice cream with our fingers, you know," Athena teased. She daintily placed the napkin in her lap.

Evelyn followed her example. It occurred to her that she had an awful lot to learn about civilized society if she were going to be half as gracious as her newfound friend.

"A word to the wise," Athena said. "Eat slowly or it will give you a headache. Like this." She delicately dipped her spoon into the ice cream and scooped up a small amount, then brought the spoon to her mouth. "Mmmmmmmmmm."

Evelyn did everything exactly the same. The aroma of the chocolate made her mouth water before she even had a taste. When she put the spoon in her mouth, the cold, the taste, the velvet smoothness, were unlike any food she had ever tasted. "Oh my."

"Can you see why I adore it?" Athena asked with a girlish twinkle. "Imagine having some with every meal."

"It would be heaven." Evelyn closed her eyes and let her second spoonful melt in her mouth.

"You're quite the little charmer," Athena said. "Your parents are fortunate. I've always wanted a daughter, but it's out of the question."

"All you need is a husband."

Athena grinned. "And sometimes not even that. But no, I meant that literally. I've been to several doctors, the best money can afford, and they all told me the same thing." She lowered her spoon and grew downcast. "I can never have children, Evelyn. Ever."

"I'm sorry for you."

Athena brightened a little. "You sound sincere."

"I am. No one likes to see another person sad."

"Quite remarkable," Athena said.

"What is?"

"You." Athena resumed eating. "So where are your parents? I would very much like to meet them and congratulate them on raising such an exceptional young woman."

Evelyn felt her ears grow warm. "Shucks, I'm nothing special." She paused to savor more ice cream. "I'm here with my uncle and aunt who aren't really my uncle and aunt, but we've called them that since we were knee-high to grasshoppers."

"Your father and mother have passed on?"

"Oh, no. They're both alive. But my father was hurt and my mother is nursing him so Uncle Shakespeare brought me here and—" Evelyn stopped. A breathless bellboy had rushed up to their table and was waiting for the chance to speak.

Athena was suddenly different. Her face became as hard as flint and she showed no interest in her ice cream. "What did you find out?"

"I spoke to him in person, ma'am, just as you wanted. He says he never got their names. They rode off without telling him."

"He has no idea where they went? Where they are staying?"

"No, ma'am. But he said for a hundred dollars

he's willing to find them for you. He has contacts all over town."

Athena considered that, then told the bellboy, "I'll have someone else do it. Go on about your own business. If I have further need of you, I'll let you know."

"Yes ma'am."

Evelyn waited until the bellboy was gone, then asked, "Is everything all right? You seem upset."

"It's nothing, my dear. A minor setback. But I'll overcome it. I always do." Athena picked up her spoon. "Now, let's finish this ice cream before it melts."

"If it does we should order a second bowl."

"Someone who knows what she wants out of life," Athena said, winking. "In some respects you're a lot like me."

Evelyn had never felt more flattered.

Chapter Twelve

There were days, many of them, when Zach King wondered what purpose females served other than to make males miserable. Every female he ever knew, every single one, had at one time or another done things that made him want to pull his hair out in frustration.

When Zach was little it was his mother who had a disturbing knack for aggravating him no end.

She always made him clean up after himself and wash his own buckskins and keep his hair tangle-free. She wouldn't let him go off into the forest on his own unless he told her where he was going and how long he would be gone. She stopped him from decimating the chipmunks and squirrels in the vicinity of their cabin even after he assured her he was only doing it for target practice. And on and on it went.

Then there was Zach's little sister. She was forever teasing and taunting and generally doing what she could to make his jaw muscles twitch. He would forget to do a chore and she would tell on him. He would leave his clothes lying where he shouldn't or leave a mess at the table and she was quick to inform their parents. When he was practicing with his guns or his knife or his tomahawk and missed, she would laugh and mention how the Blackfeet had nothing to worry about if they attacked. And on and on it went.

Then there was Louisa. Some days she was the sweetest woman alive. Other days she made him question whether taking her as his wife was the smartest thing he ever did or the dumbest. She could be kind and supportive one minute, carping at him the next. Pick up his clothes. Chew with his mouth shut. Don't leave his weapons lying on the floor. Clean the floor when he spilled something. Don't put his cold feet against her legs at night. Don't kiss her hair right after eating honey. Don't wake her up by pulling on her nipples. And on and on it went.

Shortly before the incident with the Borkes, Zach had talked with his father about it. He approached Nate one day while Nate was chopping firewood and bluntly asked, "Why do women do the things they do?"

Nate had stopped swinging his big double-edged axe and leaned on the handle. "What now?"

"I want to head back to our cabin, but Lou wants to stay here another three or four days to help Ma make that quilt."

"You don't like our company?"

"It's not that," Zach said. "I found sign of a bull elk in our valley and I want to get him before he heads up into the high country. It would save me a lot of hunting later on and supply us with enough meat to last months. Lou knows that. But she won't see things my way."

"Marriage is about give and take," his father had said.

"But why do we do all the giving and they do all the taking?"

Nate had mopped his brow, then said, "Women do as much giving as men. More, I'd say, since they give of their bodies so we can walk around with a smile on our face. And never forget what a woman goes through when she gives birth. The sickness. The pain. If that's not giving, I don't know what is."

Zach remembered sighing and shaking his head. "I should have known better than to ask you. You're always trying to understand both sides of things."

"Isn't that what we should do?"

"I suppose," Zach reluctantly conceded. But deep down he had a suspicion he would never be as understanding and considerate as his father. They were different, Nate and he, in a lot of ways. His temper, for example. Zach was quick to anger, his father exceedingly slow. But once his father *was* mad, look out. Riling Nate King was worse than riling a wolverine.

All this went through Zach's head while he reclined on the sofa waiting for his wife to return. He figured the best thing to do was apologize. He would humor her and spend the night at the hotel, and maybe, just maybe, she would be in such a good mood, they would make the night *really* memorable.

The minutes crawled by and became half an hour. Zach grew impatient. He stood at the window and watched the people in the street go by. Lou didn't show. He waited another twenty minutes, then strapped her knife around his waist, slid her pistols under his belt, grabbed her Hawken and ammo pouch and powder horn, and went out. His armory went unnoticed. Many people went about armed, but few with more weapons than he had.

Zach glanced both directions, then turned left. He had a hunch where she had gone. It felt good to be on the move, to be doing something. Zach never liked being cooped up. As a child he would get cabin fever after two days. Winters, with their heavy snows and fierce cold that kept the family indoors for a month at a stretch, had been the time of year he hated most. Now, after weeks in an army stockade, he yearned for the wide open spaces, for the prairie and the mountains, for the sky as his roof and the earth as his bed.

Suddenly a woman stepped from a recessed doorway and caught hold of his sleeve. "Hold on there, handsome."

Zach nearly struck her. She was twice his age, with baggy cheeks and a double chin and a dress much too tight. She also reeked of liquor. "What do you want?"

The woman grinned and winked. "What do you think? How about a tumble for a dollar?"

"How about you breathe on someone else." Zach tried to go, but she clung to his arm.

"Not even for a paltry dollar? I promise to make it worth your while. I've got more experience than any girl in town."

"I'm married," Zach informed her.

"So?" She winked again. "I won't tell if you won't." She pulled him toward the doorway. "Come on. What do you say?"

"I say that if you don't let go this instant, I'll slit your throat from ear to ear." Zach didn't mean it. He would never cut her. Punch her, yes, and stomp on her a few times, but not cut her.

"Bastard," the woman grumbled, and stepped back. "You should be grateful. Not many gals will look twice at a redskin."

Simmering with anger, Zach strode on. She was typical of whites. Typical of how they imposed themselves on others with no regard for anyone's feelings. Everything was about *them, them, them.* That was on top of the rancid taint of their constant bigotry. The looks they gave him, the thinly veiled hatred and contempt, were almost more than he could endure.

Zach was amazed he had married a white girl. All those years of despising them—except for the good ones like his father and Shakespeare and some others he could think of—and he went and fell in love with someone who belonged to the race that hated him so deeply.

His mother once told him that love could never be defined or denied. At the time he had not understood, but now he thought he did. He loved Lou with all his heart, but he could never describe why. Nor could he deny his affection. It flowed from him as naturally as breath flowed from his lungs. Something about her, something as rare and as precious as gold, stirred him deep inside in ways no one else ever had.

In one of his father's books Zach once read that love was like having one's heart pierced by an arrow. A true observation in his case. Love had struck with the suddenness of a thunderclap, and never once had he regretted it.

The sight of The Armistead brought Zach out of his reverie. He started to cross the street, then wheeled and went down an alley to the rear. Maybe there really were Good Samaritans in the world who went around reserving hotel suites for total strangers out of the kindness of their hearts, but he couldn't shake his suspicion that something was amiss. And if this Good Samaritan was white, as the lawyer had led them to believe, then it made the offer all the more suspect.

Which was why Zach decided to exercise caution and sneak in through the rear. The door was unlocked. He thought there would be stairs but there weren't. A short hall brought him to a kitchen where a man in an apron was chopping celery and another was busy at an oven. Both had their backs to him. He made it past them undetected.

Now Zach had his choice of two hallways. At the end of one was a dining area. He followed the other hallway. It brought him to a door that opened into the lobby.

Several people were lounging about, reading newspapers or talking. The ones who interested Zach were the desk clerk and the bellboy. The former was placing letters into slots; the latter was drinking a glass of water.

Zach was between the front desk and the stairs. Someone was bound to spot him if he tried to slip up the stairs from the bottom. But he had a better idea. Taking several quick steps he coiled and leaped straight up with his arms outstretched. It was the work of a moment to grab the rail and swing himself up and over. Crouching, he scanned the lobby. No one had seen him. He took the steps two at a time until he came to the first landing.

A middle-aged couple approached. Zach worried his buckskins and guns would alarm them, but they smiled and nodded so he did the same.

Climbing swiftly to the third floor, Zach read the numbers on the doors. Suite 304, the lawyer had said. He was set to knock since Lou had the key, but surprising her appealed to him more. He tried the door. It was unlocked.

Ducking inside, Zach quietly shut the door behind him. A cart sat nearby. On it was a bottle of wine and a card: *Courtesy of the management.*

None of the lamps were lit and the curtains were drawn, which suited Zach just fine. Grinning, he padded toward the bedrooms.

"I wish you would reconsider, Mrs. King," Major Bannister said.

"Call me Lou," Lou responded. "I'm not going to The Armistead without them, and that's final."

They were a block from her apartment and Lou was watching the window for signs of Zach.

"I don't mean that. I mean this whole business about using yourself as the bait. We should ask your husband's opinion."

He had a point. The right thing to do was tell Zach about the Borke woman. But Lou did not want him rubbing her nose in her gullibility. "We've already been through this. I *don't* want him to know. I *do* want my pistols and my rifle, though. Only an idiot waltzes into a bear's den unarmed. Wait for me."

Lou slowly climbed the stairs. To her surprise

the door was locked. She inserted her key and quietly slid inside. Right away she noticed that her rifle wasn't in the corner where she had left it. Her pistols and ammo pouch and powder horn were missing, too.

Lou figured that Zach had taken them in the bedroom so she tiptoed over and glanced at the bed where she assumed he was napping. The bed was empty.

"Zach?" Lou called out. The silence confirmed what she already knew. She hurried to the door and yanked it open and nearly collided with Major Bannister. "I thought I said to wait for me."

"I refuse to go any further without talking to your husband. Maybe he can convince you that you are making a mistake."

"Ever notice how men stick up for one another?"

"Please, Mrs. King," Bannister said. "Ask your husband to step out here. He needs to be told about Athena Borke. Then we can all go to the hotel together."

"He's not here," Lou said.

"I wasn't born yesterday," the officer said, and yelled, "Mr. King? Zachary King? May I have a minute of your time?"

"I've never been so insulted in my life," Lou said, and brushed past him. Her dander was up. She refused to answer as Bannister trailed after her, asking her repeatedly to stop. Finally he grabbed her and spun her around.

"*Must* you be so pigheaded?"

"Are you married?" Lou asked him.

Bannister blinked. "No. Why?"

"I didn't think so." Lou continued walking, leaving him no choice but to join her or be left behind.

"You're taking this too lightly, Mrs. King. As a soldier I have known some deadly men in my time, and Largo impresses me as one of the deadliest. He could lift a bull over his head without half trying."

"You have your pepperbox."

"And you have your—" The major blinked again. "Where are your weapons? That was the whole purpose for the detour to your apartment."

"I imagine my husband has them and is searching for me as we speak," Lou surmised. "We'll make do without."

Bannister's jaw muscles twitched, but he held in his irritation until they rounded a corner and saw The Armistead. A carriage was pulling up. It blocked their view of the entrance.

"It's not too late to reconsider," Bannister said. "I can't guarantee I can protect you if we go any farther."

Lou was patient with him. "Major, I've lived in the Rockies for years. I've had grizzlies try to eat me. I've had hostiles try to turn me into a pincushion. I've been kidnapped and shot at. One time my horse stepped in a prairie dog hole and broke its leg, and I had to walk for two days to reach our cabin."

"Your point?"

Lou's patience ran out. "I can protect myself quite well without help from anyone." She pointed at the hotel. "You say a woman who wants my husband dead might be waiting in there for him. I say we go in and find out, and if she's there, I'll borrow your pepperbox, and that will be that."

"You can't kill someone in cold blood," Major Bannister said.

"She intends to kill Zach and me. I'm only doing as Scripture teaches. An eye for an eye, remember?"

"It also teaches something else. Those who live by the sword will die by the sword."

Before Lou could reply, a window on the third floor of the hotel exploded outward with a tremendous crash. She glanced up and saw a human form plummeting earthward. A form she instantly recognized.

It was Zach.

Chapter Thirteen

Zach King had checked all the rooms in suite 304 except the second bedroom. As he stood in the doorway a sense of unease came over him. He could not say what caused it, but he stopped and strained to hear the slightest sound. From outside came the clomp of hooves from a passing horse and rider. Somewhere in The Armistead a baby was crying. But that was all.

Zach leveled the Hawken and took a cautious

step. He felt much as he had the time he had been about to explore a cave in the Rockies and sensed something was amiss. A roar had reverberated through the cavern, and a female grizzly came charging out of the darkness. He'd dodged behind a boulder and the mother bear and her cubs barreled on by and went off down the mountain. Fortunately for him. No creature in all creation was more fierce than a mother bear protecting her offspring.

Zach scanned the bedroom. It was much like the first one: a bed, a vanity, carpeted floor, the curtains drawn. He was about to go farther when the reason for his uneasiness dawned on him. It had to do with the window. With the drawn curtains. Every single window was the same. He had been to a few hotels with his parents, and the curtains in those had always been left open so the room was bright and airy.

The only explanation Zach could think of was that maybe no one had used the suite in a while and someone on the staff had closed the curtains to keep out the dust.

Zach warily moved toward the middle of the room. His feeling of uneasiness grew. He studied the bed but could find nothing out of the ordinary. It had been made to perfection. The pillows had been fluffed, the quilt was flat and unruffled.

Slowly easing onto one knee, Zach used the Hawken to lift the bottom edge of the quilt high enough to see under the bed. No one was there.

The vanity was too close to the wall for anyone

to hide behind it. That left the closet, which was cracked open a few inches.

Zach started around the bed, then stopped again. The inside of the closet was darker than the room. That was to be expected. But there was a patch of black even darker than the rest, a hint that someone or something was in there. "Come out with your hands where I can see them, or I will shoot through the door."

Time crawled by on snail's feet. Zach was about convinced he was making a fool of himself when the closet door was slowly pushed all the way open and a gigantic shape unfurled from within. It rose toward the ceiling, its arms out to either side. He had never seen anyone so huge.

"You've caught me," the words rumbled from the giant's chest, and he smiled. "I'm impressed. How did you know I was in there?"

"Your silhouette," Zach said.

"Your eyesight is extraordinary," the man complimented him.

"Who are you and what are you doing here?"

"I'm a thief," the man said. "I was looking for things to steal when I heard you come in."

"I didn't make any noise."

"My senses are extraordinary too," the man said. He wasn't boasting, just stating a fact. "What now?"

"I'm taking you downstairs to the desk clerk." Zach would let the hotel staff deal with the intruder.

"Why go to all that bother? You caught me before I could take anything." When Zach did not reply right away the big man said, "I haven't stolen anything of yours, haven't harmed you in any way. Let me go my way and you go yours."

There was something about the way the man said it, something about his expression, that made Zach suspect there was more involved. This was, after all, the room the "Good Samaritan" had reserved for Lou and him. He motioned. "Step around the bed and head down the hall." He backed to the wall to give the other man plenty of room.

"Come on, mister. Be reasonable." The man in black smiled. "What is this hotel to you that you should care? Let me go. I promise you'll never set eyes on me again."

"Start walking."

"Is it because I'm a thief? I only do it because I'm down on my luck. Haven't you ever stolen anything?"

No, Zach hadn't. His father had impressed on him from an early age that stealing was wrong. The Shoshones frowned on it too, among their own people. Stealing a horse or gun from an enemy, though, were praiseworthy feats. "For a man down on his luck, you wear mighty nice clothes."

"I could be hanged," the big man said. "Would you let someone's neck be stretched for something so trivial?"

"When did stealing become a hanging offense?" Zach could tell the man was stalling. "Enough talk. Stay in front of me and don't try anything."

The man's broad shoulders slumped and he started around the bed. "I guess I have this coming for being so stupid. Since I've never run into anyone who can hold their own against me, I take it for granted no one can. That's a mistake."

Zach disliked the ceaseless chatter and was about to tell the so-called thief to shut up when the man did a remarkable thing. Exhibiting startling speed, he bent and grabbed the quilt and in a single wrench ripped it off the bed and flung it straight at him. Zach tried to dart to one side, but the quilt fell across his shoulders and wrapped itself around him. Before he knew it, he could barely move. He grabbed a fold to tear off the quilt, but bands of iron encircled his chest, pinning his arms, and he was hoisted into the air until they were nose to nose.

"You're good, boy. I'll give you that."

Zach swore the man was looking at him with a strange mixture of respect and something else.

"To be honest, I never liked Artemis or Phineas all that much. They always treated me with contempt because I'm an indentured servant. If they ever suspected the truth they'd have shot me."

Zach struggled, but the other's strength was prodigious.

"Just so you know, my mistress wants you alive. That's the only reason I haven't crushed you."

Zach tried to get at his knife, but it was buried in folds of the quilt. Now he was the one who needed to stall. "So this was a trap?"

"My mistress wants vengeance for her brothers.

I have no personal stake in this other than carrying out her wishes."

"I heard a rumor of a sister," Zach said. "Three pups and they all turned out rotten."

The big man glowered. "You would be well advised to speak of my mistress with respect. I will no more tolerate insults to her than you would tolerate an insult to your wife." He gazed toward the hall. "Where is she, by the way?"

"Safe from you," Zach said. By then he was ready. Snapping his head back, he butted the man on the jaw, not once but twice. It was like slamming his forehead against an anvil. For a few moments pinpoints of light flickered before him. But it had the desired effect.

The man in black staggered. His grip slackened. Not a lot, but enough for Zach to give a powerful heave of both arms and break free. He tripped and fell against the wall but stayed on his feet and the next moment he had shrugged the quilt off. He attempted to level the Hawken.

A hand as huge as a haunch of venison gripped the barrel. Zach clung to the stock and was jerked to his knees. A foot twice of the size of his flashed at his face. Dropping onto his shoulder, Zach rolled toward the door. He never made it. Fingers as strong as steel dug into his shoulders and he was heaved off the floor and thrown against the wall with bone-jarring force. His rifle went flying.

"Don't make this harder than it has to be, boy," his attacker calmly said. "I don't want to hurt you any more than is necessary. My mistress reserves that honor." He bent forward, his huge hands opening.

Dodging, Zach swung a looping right that caught the man on the neck. Not hard enough to crush the other's jugular, but it caused him to clutch his throat and take a step back, grunting in pain.

Zach grabbed one of his pistols. As it cleared his belt his wrist was gripped in an inhumanly strong vise. For a few moments he thought the bone would shatter. The pain was excruciating. Involuntarily, he let go. Those same steel fingers seized him by the front of his buckskin shirt and he was raised almost to the ceiling, then slammed to the floor.

The carpet spared Zach from being gravely hurt. As it was, the room spun and he nearly blacked out. Scrambling to one side, he reached his knees just as the man in black reached him.

"Why won't you stay down?"

Again Zach was lifted into the air. This time he aimed a punch at the other's face and connected with a cheek. It was not enough. Once again he was brutally slammed to the floor.

"I should have known," the giant said.

Zach made a stab for his other pistol. He thrust out his arm and thumbed back the hammer, but a new vise was applied to his wrist and his elbow, and his arm was nearly wrenched from its socket. Again he had no choice but to let the gun fall.

"You can't win. No one has ever beaten me."

"There's a first time for everything," Zach said.

He still had Lou's knife, and drawing it, he lunged. The man in black skipped from his reach and suddenly was holding a Bowie. Their blades met, separated, met again, the ring of metal-on-metal loud in the confines of the bedroom.

The giant circled. "Poor choice of weapons, boy. I've killed a score of men with my blade."

The Bowie flicked at Zach's eye, but he tucked at the knees and lanced his knife into his adversary's redwood-thick thigh. It bit deep, and he danced out of the way of the Bowie.

Taking a long step back, the giant looked down, then at Zach. His eyes showed white in the dark. Not the white of fear but the white of red-hot rage. "If my mistress didn't want you for herself—" He closed in, weaving the Bowie in a glittering display of superb skill.

Zach parried, shifted, countered, spun away. He was hard pressed to keep from being stabbed or cut. Several times he attempted to reach the door, but the giant was always right there, always pressing him, as relentless as an avalanche.

It hit Zach that the man in black wasn't trying to kill him but to disarm him and take him alive. But Zach had some skill with a knife himself, and he would be damned if he let the other prevail.

Suddenly the big man sprang back out of reach. "You continue to surprise me. You have real talent. But not enough. We both know how this will end."

"With you dead or behind bars?" Zach said. "All I have to do is yell and people will come running."

"You won't," the other said smugly. "You're not the kind to call for help."

"I might surprise you," Zach said. But the man was right. He fought his own fights. Feinting, he speared his knife at the giant's other leg. This time, though, the manservant was ready. Their blades met, parted, met again. Whirling, slashing, always in motion, Zach sought to exploit lapses in the other's guard. But there was none.

Suddenly they were next to the vanity and the chair.

Without a heartbeat's hesitation, Zach grabbed the chair and flung it. His foe swatted it to the floor with no more effort than it would take Zach to swat a mosquito.

It bought Zach the seconds he needed to whirl and dart from the bedroom. He came to the main room and spun. The man in black was almost on top of him. Once more their blades rang. Each time their knives made contact, Zach's arm was spiked by pain. There was no denying the other man was far stronger. Even so, newfound confidence flowed through Zach's veins. He had realized something; the giant was stronger but Zach was a shade faster.

Maybe the man in black was winded, Zach thought. Or maybe it was the thigh wound and loss of blood. Whatever the reasons, his swings were not as quick, his parries had lost some of their power.

Zach leaped to the offensive. He was no longer just trying to stay alive; he was out for blood, out to kill. He was a Shoshone warrior with an overwhelming urge to count coup, and he would not be denied.

The giant was limping. Twice he put his free hand to his thigh, but each time he had to remove it to ward off Zach's flurries. He was also breathing heavily.

Zach faked a stab to the left, pivoted, and stabbed to the right, opening his enemy's forearm. Not deeply, but the man backed off and stared at the cut and growled deep in his chest. "Damn you, King. That's twice now. There won't be a third time." He set himself. "My mistress will be upset with me, but it can't be helped. It's you or me and it won't be me."

"Are you sure?" Zach taunted.

"I'll gut you and strangle you with your own intestines."

The man renewed his assault with a ferocity Zach could never hope to match. Once more he was on the defensive. Blocking attempt after attempt to end his life, he slowly backed up until he bumped against the cart with the wine bottle.

Grabbing the bottle, Zach kicked the cart and sent it rolling at the other's legs. The man moved nimbly aside but not quickly enough. The cart struck his wounded leg and he staggered and nearly toppled.

Instantly Zach sprang. The giant looked up just as Zach brought the wine bottle crashing down onto his head. Glass shattered into a hundred fragments and red wine splashed them both.

For most men, breaking a bottle over their head

would be enough to knock them out. But not this one. The big man teetered, regained his balance, and retaliated with a vicious swing that came within a hairsbreadth of cleaving Zach's head from his shoulders.

Zach backpedaled.

Roaring like an incensed beast, the man fought like a madman. He swung the Bowie from right to left and left to right, from high to low and low to high.

It was only by the grace of God and his wilderness-honed reflexes that Zach kept the Grim Reaper at bay. Backing against a table, he shoved it out of his way. Only he shoved too hard and the table upended instead, and in doing so, its legs became entangled with his. He tried to stay upright but couldn't.

In a bound the Goliath reached him. Zach's arms were seized and he was whipped violently about, first in one one direction, then another. Zach aimed a kick that connected with the other's knee. A hiss escaped the giant's lips. He pushed with all his might.

Zach braced for impact with the wall. But he struck something softer. The curtains, as it turned out, which were not enough to slow him down and stop him from striking the window itself. He clutched for the jamb, but then cool air was on his face and he dropped like a rock toward the ground three stories below.

Chapter Fourteen

Shakespeare McNair was adrift on a tranquil lake. Not in a canoe or bull-hide boat, but floating serenely on his back, a blue sky overhead, a gentle breeze caressing his face and beard. He felt a sense of supreme peace.

Shakespeare was content to drift in bliss forever. Restful interludes like this were all too rare. In the Rockies life was a never-ending struggle for existence. Predators and hostiles posed a constant threat. A person must never let his vigilance lapse or it could prove fatal.

The soft rhythmic lapping of the water was melodious to Shakespeare's ears. He didn't wonder how it was he could be floating in water and still be dry, or how he got in the lake. He only knew he was happy. He only knew he did not want anything to spoil the moment. So naturally something did.

It started as a bleat in the distance, like the cry of a lost lamb, and grew gradually louder. Someone was saying the same words over and over, and began shaking his shoulder.

"—up, husband. Wake up."

Shakespeare cracked his eyes open, and sighed. "Away, wench, or I'll sic the three witches from Macbeth on you."

"Evelyn has been gone a long time. I thought you would want to know."

"Define 'long time,'" Shakespeare said. He closed his eyes, but the lake and the gentle breeze had faded into the inner limbo that spawned them.

"Almost an hour by your pocket watch," Blue Water Woman said. "Do you want me to go look for her?"

"You are too absolute," Shakespeare quoted, "though therein you can never be too noble." Sitting up, he rubbed his beard and ran a hand through his hair. "We don't want you lifting the scalps of any locals."

"You're the one with the temper," Blue Water Woman said.

"Few love to hear the sins they love to act." Shakespeare slid his legs over the edge of the bed. "I'll bet Evelyn is doing what I would do at her age, and exploring the hotel."

"What if she has left the hotel to explore the town?"

"We told her not to." Shakespeare stretched and stifled a yawn.

"But if she is as much like you as you believe," Blue Water Woman said, "she will listen to us about as well as you listen to me."

"This to the man who hangs on your every word?" Shakespeare stood. "She is her father's daughter, though. So maybe we better go see." Padding to the wash basin, he splashed water on his face and gave his head a vigorous shake. "There. I think I'm awake enough for the hunt."

They stepped from the bedroom and were almost to the front door when the wall shook to a resounding *thump*.

"What was that?" Blue Water Woman wondered.

"An irate storm giant," Shakespeare joked.

From the next suite came loud scuffling noises and a tinny *kling-kling-kling*.

Blue Water Woman commented, "That sounds like silverware on a tin plate."

"Thou art so leaky that we must leave thee to thy sinking," Shakespeare recited the Bard, and placed an ear to the wall. "That's a knife fight or I'm a urinal." He thought he heard a grunt and then indistinct voices.

"Maybe you should let the hotel people know."

Shakespeare agreed. Knife fights sometimes ended in the use of firearms, and the walls weren't thick enough to stop a stray slug. "Good idea. I'll run right down."

"We will go together. We are husband and wife, in case you have forgotten."

"How can I when we've been joined at the hip since the day I gave in?" Shakespeare said. He already had his pistols, knife and tomahawk. All he needed was his rifle, which he had propped by the door.

Another couple was in the hallway, young lovers or newlyweds, from the way they clung to one another.

"Do you hear that?" the young man asked. "What in the world is going on in there?"

"A dance of death would be my guess," Shakespeare replied. "Juliet and you should make your-selves scarce, Romeo."

"My name is Cynthia," the young woman said.

"Of course it is," Shakespeare said.

Timms, the desk clerk, was watering a plant. "Mr. McNair? Mrs. McNair? Why the hurry and the furrowed brows? Don't tell me there is a prob-lem with your suite?"

"There's a fight in the one next to us," Shake-speare said. "Three-oh-four, I think it is."

"A fight? At The Armistead?" Timms chuckled. "Unthinkable. In the year I've been here there has never been an altercation. People who stay here do so for a taste of the rich life, not to indulge in petty fisticuffs."

"If our wits run the wild goose chase I am done, for thou hast more of the wild goose in one of thy wits than I am sure I have in my whole five."

"I beg your pardon?"

Shakespeare was not one to suffer simpletons, and he turned, saying, "It must be nice to be part ostrich."

"You're serious about the fight?" Timms said.

Suddenly a tremendous crash drew everyone in the lobby to the wide double doors. Across the street someone screamed.

A man at the front window pointed in amaze-ment. "Look! Someone just fell from an upper win-dow. My God! Every bone in his body must be broken!"

Shakespeare pulled Blue Water Woman over to see who it was. He felt her stiffen, and he stiffened, too, his mind reeling at the impossibility of the evidence of his eyes. "It can't be!"

But it was.

Lying in the dust of the street, his limbs spread-eagled, was the firebrand they had traveled a thousand miles to help, the grandson Shakespeare never had but always wanted, one of the five people he loved most in the world: Zachary King.

Evelyn finished her ice cream and placed her spoon in the bowl. "That was delicious, ma'am," she thanked her gracious benefactor.

"Would you care for more?"

"Oh, no, I couldn't," Evelyn said to be polite. She wouldn't mind another two or three bowls. It was that good.

Athena glanced at the waiter and he hurried to their table. "Put them on my bill," she directed.

"Of course, madam."

Evelyn had never met anyone like her. She never imagined a woman could be so forceful, so commanding. Her mother was a strong woman but not in the way Athena was strong. One day she would like to be just like her. "I sure do envy you."

"And I you, little one."

"I have nothing to envy," Evelyn said.

"On the contrary, my dear. You have the most precious gift life offers. Your youth. We squander it when we are children, miss it when we are old."

"But you're still young yet."

Athena smiled and reached across the table and touched Evelyn's chin. "I thank you for the kindness. But you cannot always tell someone's age by how they look. Appearances, you might have heard, can be deceiving." She nodded at the waiter and he held her chair out for her. "Often how old we are has more to do with how we feel inside, not how we appear in a mirror."

"You're saying you feel older than you are?"

"I may only look thirty, but at times I feel one hundred," Athena said. "Hardship and loss have turned me ancient beyond my years." She moved toward the lobby but stopped after only a few steps. "This is where we part company. I have things to attend to, and I would imagine your uncle and aunt are wondering what became of you." She held out her hand. "Thank you for your company."

"My pleasure."

Athena began to leave, then turned back. "I almost forgot. You never mentioned your last name. What if I want to look you up later?"

"King," Evelyn said. "My full name is Evelyn King."

Athena recoiled as if she had been pricked by a pin. "Can it be?" she breathed. "Are you any relation to Zach King?"

Evelyn remembered all those who hated her brother because he was half and half, and she timidly replied, "I'm his sister. Why?"

"But you don't look anything like him! Your hair, your eyes, your complexion. No one would guess you are part Indian."

"You've met him?"

"Not personally yet, no," Athena said, "but I followed his trial with great interest. How is it I never saw you there?"

"We just got into town today," Evelyn disclosed. "I wanted to be here for him, but we were delayed out on the prairie."

"Then you haven't seen your brother yet?"

"No." Evelyn couldn't understand why Athena glanced all around. "We don't even know where he is."

"I do. I happened to overhear someone mention it during the course of the trial." Athena leaned down and cupped Evelyn's cheek. "I can take you to him right this second if you want."

"Take all three of us, you mean," Evelyn said. "Uncle Shakespeare and Aunt Blue Water Woman will want to come too."

"Of course, of course." Athena took Evelyn's hand. "Come with me." Hardly had she taken a step than there was a loud crash and a scream from in front of the hotel, and a commotion erupted.

"What's going on?" Evelyn asked. Athena was blocking her view. "What is all the ruckus about?"

A man shouted, "Look! Someone just fell from an upper window. My God! Every bone in his body must be broken!"

"Evidently there has been a terrible accident." Athena moved toward the stairs, her arm around Evelyn's shoulder, walking on the right so Evelyn couldn't see.

"I'm not squeamish," Evelyn remarked, trying to catch a glimpse. A crowd was gathering in the street and there had to be ten to twelve people jammed together near the front doors. She thought she glimpsed a man with white hair but she couldn't be sure it was Shakespeare and in a few more seconds they reached the first landing. "What's our hurry?"

"You want to see your brother, don't you? I must get a few things and we'll be on our way."

"Don't forget my uncle and my aunt," Evelyn reminded her.

"Don't fret on that score."

Athena produced a key and went to insert it into a door, but the door wasn't locked and swung open at her touch. Just inside, on the floor, was a bright red smear. "What—?" she blurted.

"Blood," Evelyn said. "I've seen enough of it to know." The most recent incident was the mauling of her father by the black bear. He had bled so much, her mother and Shakespeare feared he would die from blood loss.

Athena pulled her into the suite and shut and bolted the door. "I need to change. Then we'll go."

More red smears sprinkled the carpet. On the sofa sat one of the biggest men Evelyn ever saw. He was even bigger than Touch the Clouds, and that took some doing. He was dressed all in black except for his shirt. His leg was bleeding. He had a belt around it to stop the flow.

"Mistress! All did not go as—" The man saw Evelyn and stopped. "Who is the girl?"

"She is living proof that God answers our

prayers. Permit me to introduce Miss Evelyn King, Zach King's younger sister. Evelyn, meet Largo, my manservant."

"Can it be?" Largo marveled. "After all we—" Again he stopped. "There has been an unforeseen development."

"Come into your bedroom and I will bandage you," Athena said. To Evelyn she said, "Will you be so kind as to wait here? We won't be long, and then I will take you to your brother."

"I can hardly wait."

Evelyn settled into a chair. She was curious how the big man had hurt himself, but she could wait to find out. The important thing was to get to Zach. She would never admit it to his face, but she missed him. When he'd been arrested by the army, she couldn't sleep for days. Oh, sure, they had fought a lot when she was little, but she still cared for him. She still loved him.

Athena and Largo closed the bedroom door and commenced whispering excitedly. Evelyn thought she heard her name and Zach's and something about New Orleans. They were in there a long time and when they came out Athena wore a hat with a veil and Largo had changed into a clean pair of pants with a slight bulge where the bandage had been applied.

"Will you take me to my brother now?" Evelyn requested.

"Soon. Very soon," Athena said. "But first we need to know which room your uncle and aunt are staying in."

Evelyn told them, and Athena nodded at Largo, who quickly departed. "Where is he going?"

"To ask them to accompany us." Athena came over to the chair, her left hand low against her side. "You have no idea how much our chance meeting means to me."

"It does?" Evelyn saw a crumpled cloth in Athena's left hand and assumed it was one Athena had used to doctor her servant.

"Were I religious, I would say the Almighty dropped you in my lap to do with as I please."

"Ma'am?" Evelyn said.

"Breathe deep, my dear."

Evelyn was stupefied when Athena abruptly grabbed her and pressed the cloth to her mouth and nose. For a few seconds she was too stunned to move. When she did, when she sought to rise and run, her body wouldn't obey. A sickening dizziness came over her. She heard laughter, cold, hard laughter, right before the world faded to black.

Chapter Fifteen

A cool sensation on Zach King's forehead was his first inkling he was still alive. He opened his eyes and winced when his head exploded with excruciating pain. He was lying on his back. He raised a hand to his brow and discovered a damp, folded cloth.

"Doctor! He's come around!"

A face Zach had never seen before appeared above him. "Who—?" he croaked, trying to collect his jumbled thoughts.

"Lie still, young man. You've sustained a blow to the head. I'm Dr. Peters. Your wife sent for me."

"Where—?" Zach said, then saw the glittering chandelier. He was in the lobby of The Armistead.

"You fell from the third floor," Dr. Peters said. "The only thing that saved you from a broken neck or worse was a carriage that had pulled up."

Zach remembered. It was one of those carriages with a soft leather top. He had struck it, bounced off, and crashed headfirst to the street.

"You must lie still for a while," Dr. Peters advised. "Concussions are common in falls of this nature." He pried at one of Zach's eyelids and carefully examined the eye. "Your pupils aren't dilated." Holding up three fingers, he asked, "How many fingers do you see?"

Zach told him.

Dr. Peters took the folded cloth. "I'll get another cold compress. They'll help with the discomfort."

Lou's face replaced the doctor's. She had tears in her eyes. Throwing her arms wide, she embraced him and pressed her cheek to his. "Oh, Zach, Zach, Zach. I thought I had lost you."

"It was close," Zach admitted. "Was that you who screamed?" He vaguely remembered it being the last sound he heard before he passed out.

Lou nodded. "I was never so scared in my life," she said, kissing him. A sheepish look came over her and she drew back. "We carried you into the lobby."

Where a lot of people had congregated, Zach now saw. He was on a couch, surrounded by gawkers, two of whom he recognized. "Shakespeare! Blue Water Woman!" Impulsively, he went to sit up. Waves of pulsating pain drove him back down.

"Lie still, Laertes," Shakespeare said, gripping Zach's hand. "Didn't you hear the sawbones? That iron noggin of yours took quite a blow."

"We are happy to see you again," Blue Water Woman said in that reserved way of hers.

Zach glanced at the ring of faces. "Where are my father and mother?" Those long weeks he spent languishing in the stockade at Fort Leavenworth, he had looked for their arrival daily. He never understood why they weren't at the trial. They had plenty of time to make the long trek across the plains.

Shakespeare's features clouded. "Your pa is in a bad way, son. He was mauled by a black bear."

"*Again?*" When it came to bears, Zach's father had the worst luck of any man alive. As far back as Zach could remember, his father was always tangling with them. It got so that the mountaineers liked to joke that Nate had a hoodoo on him.

"We were two weeks out," Shakespeare detailed. "There was a storm, and your father and the bear were caught in a mud slide. The bear ripped him open clear to the bone, but he should live."

"Should?" Zach said bleakly.

"He sent us on ahead. We're sorry we didn't get here in time for your trial, but we tried out best."

Blue Water Woman touched Zach's shoulder. "Your mother asked me to express her regrets. She had to stay with your father. She hopes you will understand."

Zach was too choked up to answer so he nodded.

"Now that we've found you," Shakespeare said, "we're not letting you out of our sight until you're reunited with your folks." He gave a grin and added, "Someone has to keep you out of trouble."

The mention of trouble flooded Zach with images of his fight, and of being thrown through the window. "I was attacked by someone three times as big as me."

"That would be Largo Gandovar," said someone else, and out of the onlookers stepped the man in the brown hat.

"You!" Again Zach tried to rise. Again he regretted it.

"Be still," Lou said. "He's on our side. Colonel Templeton sent him to help us."

"Major Bannister, at your service," the officer said with a courteous bow. "Your wife can fill you in on all we have learned so far. In the meantime I'll go find your assailant."

"You won't go alone," Shakespeare McNair said.

"No, he won't." This time Zach made it to his feet. He swayed but only for a few moments. Pushing away Lou's restraining hand, he declared, "This is mine to deal with." Strong words when his stomach was trying to crawl up out his throat.

Shakespeare shook his head. "We'll handle it, Laertes. There's no need for you to come."

"Would you do nothing if someone tried to kill *you*?" Zach countered. A question for which the oldest of the mountaineers had no answer. Helping himself to one of McNair's pistols, he said, "I need to borrow this."

The onlookers parted and through them came Dr. Peters holding the wet cloth. "What are you doing on your feet? Didn't you hear a word I said? You must rest."

"There's something that needs doing first, Doc." Zach shuffled a step, then several more. With each one the throbbing in his head lessened and more of his strength returned.

From behind the front desk came a thin-faced man in a starched shirt and jacket who barred his way. "A moment of your time, Mr. King, if I may. I'm Harold Timms, the desk clerk."

"Stand aside," Zach said. He had to get upstairs before Largo escaped, if he hadn't already.

"I've sent a bellboy to the manager's house," Timms said. "Here at The Armistead we frown on escapades of this nature. What were you doing here, anyhow? And who is going to pay for any damages?"

"I'll answer everything later." Zach pressed the pistol's muzzle against Timms's chest. "Right now the man who tried to kill me might still be upstairs. So move."

Timms had more grit than Zach credited him with. "You won't shoot me in front of all these witnesses."

"No," Zach concurred. "But beating you senseless will do as well." He hefted the flintlock and Timms scampered out of reach. Concerned someone else would try to stop him, he ran to the stairs. They seemed to go on forever. He had to hold on to the rail and at each landing he paused to let the pounding subside, but eventually he reached the third floor. He wasn't alone. Lou and Shakespeare and Blue Water Woman were there to back him. Major Bannister had tagged along. So had the doctor and the desk clerk and a dozen others.

The door to Suite 304 was closed. His back to the wall, Zach sidled forward. He tried the door but it was locked. He faced it and raised his leg to kick it in, but Harold Timms materialized, holding a ring of keys.

"Please, Mr. King. Restrain yourself. There's no need to resort to so drastic a measure when I have the master keys." Timms opened the door. "There. And nothing was damaged in the process."

Shouldering past, Zach gripped the pistol in both hands to steady his aim. The hammering in his head just would not stop.

"This room is a shambles!" Timms exclaimed. "And what's this stain on the floor? Blood?" He touched a wet spot. "My word! It is!"

Shakespeare entered with his rifle leveled. "Try not to faint. And find somewhere else to stand. I wouldn't want to shoot you by mistake."

Lou glued herself to Zach's elbow as he warily approached the bedrooms. Their eyes met and she grinned. Shoulder-to-shoulder they entered the first bedroom, but it was empty. The same with the second.

Keen disappointment filled Zach even though he expected as much. He gathered up Lou's rifle and pistols from where they had fallen, and handed Shakespeare's back.

Timms was holding his head and groaning. "Have you any idea how much all this will cost?"

"I was defending myself."

"That hardly justifies destroying one of our luxury suites." Timms nodded at the window. "Half the jamb has been ripped out. Repairing it will cost close to a hundred dollars." He shook a finger at Zach. "Mark my words! There will be legal repercussions. Our attorney will demand redress in court."

"Tell that to Largo," Zach said.

Harold Timms lowered his arms. "Athena Borke's manservant? He was party to this outrage?"

"He was the one who pushed me through the window," Zach said. "The one who caused all this. Track him down and make him pay for the damages." Provided Zach didn't kill him first.

"That's not necessary," Timms said. "I know exactly where he can be found. Miss Borke's suite is just down the hall."

Major Bannister stepped up. "Athena Borke is staying here?"

"In three-oh-three," the desk clerk said. "Say. Perhaps this whole thing was a misunderstanding. Perhaps Largo entered the wrong suite by mistake and mistook Mr. King for a—"

Zach barged out the door and down the hall. He didn't wait for Timms to use a key. He tried the door, and when he found it locked, he stepped back and slammed into it. His head felt like it burst but there was a sharp *crack* and he was inside. The suite was fragrant with the scent of expensive perfume and a trace of something else, an odor new to him. He glided to the nearest bedroom. A black dress lay across the bed and other dresses hung in the closet. Two suitcases were in a corner.

"She hasn't gone yet," Lou said.

From the second bedroom came a yell from Major Bannister. "Come see what I've found!"

A wash basin filled with bloody water sat on the floor at the foot of the bed. A pair of blood-soaked towels were beside it. On the bed was the pair of pants the manservant had on when Zach stabbed him.

Bannister opened the closet. A single black suit hung inside. "Either they plan to come back or they left in such a hurry, they couldn't take their things with them."

At that juncture someone in the hall commanded, "Out of my way." Into the suite strode a short, squat man wearing a suit and boots that had seen a lot of use. His hands were shoved in his pockets, and he had a weary air about him. His blue eyes, though, were alert and bright, almost as bright as the tin star pinned to his vest. He turned to the onlookers. "I want all of you to wait in the lobby. *Don't* leave the hotel. I might need to question you."

"Marshal Owen," Major Bannister said, offering his hand. "It's a pleasure to see you again."

"Bannister?" Owen studied Zach and Lou and the McNairs. "You're involved? I had a report of a man falling from a window."

"There's much more to it than that, I'm afraid," Major Bannister said. "If you would like I can fill you in."

"I'd like," Marshal Owen said.

They moved to one side.

Timms excused himself. "The manager will be here any minute and I must be downstairs to meet him."

Zach and Lou and Shakespeare and Blue Water Woman huddled near the doorway, and Zach said, "Before any of you say anything, I'm not leaving town until this is settled. One way or the other."

"How will we find them if they do not return?" Blue Water Woman posed the problem uppermost on Zach's mind.

"The major says the Borke woman is rich as can be," Lou said. "They can go anywhere in the world and we would never find them."

Zach doubted Athena Borke would give up, not after all she'd gone through to lay her trap. "I don't like the notion of spending the rest of my life looking over my shoulder."

"We can't stay here forever," Lou said.

"Don't forget Nate and Winona," Shakespeare said. "We promised to take you to them as soon as we could."

"They'll understand," Zach said. Particulary his father, who had made a few enemies of his own.

Shakespeare turned to Louisa. "Is there room at that apartment of yours for three more? We're paid up for the night here but in the morning I'd like to move in. Safety in numbers, as they say."

"Three more?" Zach said.

"Oh. That's right. You don't know." McNair grinned. "Evelyn was worried sick about you. She begged Nate to let her tag along with us."

Blue Water Woman nodded. "Your sister will never admit it, Stalking Coyote, but she loves you dearly."

"Where is she now? In your suite?"

Shakespeare and his wife swapped puzzled glances, and Shakespeare said, "She went off exploring. With all the ruckus, you would think she'd have joined us by now."

Footsteps thudded in the hall and in rushed Harold Timms, his cheeks flushed, half out of breath. "I thought you should know right away, Mr. King."

"Know what?" Zach asked.

"While I was up here with you, a note was left at the front desk." Timms seemed reluctant to go on.

"And?" Shakespeare goaded him.

Timms thrust a folded sheet of paper at Zach. "It wasn't folded or in an envelope so when I picked it up, I read it. I couldn't believe my eyes."

The note was addressed to Zach. It was short and direct: *You will never set eyes on your sister again.*

Chapter Sixteen

Evelyn opened her eyes and was overcome by raw terror. It was pitch black. There were no sounds. She looked up, half thinking she was at the bottom of a well. Gingerly groping about, she discovered she was in a small, narrow space. Her outstretched hand bumped what she took to be a wall but seconds later the "wall" opened and Largo stared down at her as if from a great height.

"On your feet, girl, and out of the closet. My mistress has been waiting for you to revive to have words with you."

Blinking against the glare of a lamp, Evelyn rolled onto her hands and knees, crawled out, and stood. She was no longer at the hotel. The walls were made of logs, not polished mahogany, and the floor consisted of planks, not carpet. "Where am I?"

"A farmhouse my mistress rented under an assumed name the day we arrived," Largo said.

"What did she do to me? Why have you brought

me here?" Evelyn was afraid, deathly afraid, but she would not show it. Her father once told her certain hostiles tortured captives who showed fear, so she had resolved at an early age to always appear brave even when she was quaking inside.

"My mistress will answer all your questions, child." Largo indicated a door.

In a rocking chair by a stone fireplace sat Athena, dressed in a man's shirt and pants. Her long hair was tucked up under a straw hat. "So you're awake at last. I was unsure how long the chloroform would keep you under."

"The what?"

"A chemical, my dear. Veterinaries use it to put animals under, and a few doctors and dentists use it with their patients now, I understand. Obtaining some has proven well worth the expense." Athena bobbed her chin at a chair. "Have a seat. We have a lot to discuss."

"Why have you taken me?

"You must think me insane. But I assure you that nothing could be further from the truth. Abducting you will go a long way toward repaying the one responsible for the deaths of my brothers."

"Who?"

"My last name, little one, is Borke. Artemis and Phineas were my brothers." Athena let that sink in. "*Now* do you comprehend?"

Evelyn had noticed a door on the other side of the room. She gauged whether she could reach it before Largo reached her. He stood with his hands behind his back, as motionless as a statue. "You're out to get my brother?"

"I was," Athena said. "But a much more exquisite retribution has presented itself. I'm torn between killing him or having him suffer the torment of the damned for the rest of his life."

Evelyn decided she couldn't reach the door. For now she had to go along with whatever they wanted.

"When you told me your last name I could scarcely believe it," Athena was saying. "Providence delivered you into my hands."

"Do you aim to kill me?"

"That's just one of several options," Athena responded. "Our chance meeting has opened up some truly marvelous opportunities."

"Touch a hair on my head and you'll be hunted down," Evelyn predicted. "Not just by Zach, either. My folks and Uncle Shakespeare will be on your trail."

"I have heard a lot about your father. They say he has grit. That he is highly respected. And highly feared by those who have crossed him."

"My ma is respected, too. She can shoot as well as he can and has fought her share of Blackfeet and Bloods and Sioux."

"What good would all that do her in Paris or Rome? She will be in my element. At my mercy. Let her come." Athena glanced at Largo. "We have two hours yet. Heat up some tea. It will help while away the time."

"Two hours until what?" Evelyn asked.

"That is for me to know, my dear, and you to find out. If I permit you to live long enough."

"You must really hate my brother."

"Hate?" Athena's face became a twisted mask. "Hate does not begin to describe my feelings. I loathe him. I detest him. I despise him with every fiber of my being. I would like nothing better than to chop him into bits and pieces. Does that answer your question?"

"Your brothers were bad men. Artemis tried to start a war between the Shoshones and the Crows. Phineas kidnapped my Aunt Lou and would have killed her if my brother hadn't saved her."

Athena was out of the rocking chair and had seized Evelyn by the shoulders before the girl could blink. "Don't you dare!" Athena shrilly declared. "Don't you dare lecture *me* about my brothers!"

Evelyn nearly cried out when the woman's fingernails dug deep into her flesh. Gritting her teeth, she looked her tormentor in the eyes.

Gradually the color faded from Athena's cheeks and her fingers relaxed. Stepping back, she slowly sat and said, "Excuse my outburst. But I loved my brothers every bit as much as you love yours."

"I'm sorry they had to die," Evelyn said.

"*Had* to?" Athena repeated. She started to rise again but stopped. "You must choose your words more carefully, my dear."

"And you must let me go or my father and my mother and my brother and my uncle will find you and punish you."

"Empty threats mean nothing to me." Athena was silent a while, then said, "I must remember to keep in mind how young you are. You lack discretion, my dear."

"I am not your 'dear,'" Evelyn said.

"So we're not friends?" Athena laughed.

"I liked you. I trusted you. And you did this." Evelyn had seldom been as mad at anyone as she was at that moment. "I will not be sad when you die."

"Which won't be for a long time," Athena said. "I have more of a say in when that will be than you think. You forget how wealthy I am. My resources are endless. Resources I can employ to thwart your family at every turn."

"My family has tangled with the Sioux, the Blackfeet, the Apaches. We lived through blizzards and droughts. Compared to that you are nothing."

Athena leaned forward, a study in spite. "Oh, I wouldn't say that. I am your mortal enemy. The worst enemy your family has ever had. Why? Because I'm more devious than any Sioux. More vicious than any Blackfoot. The hardships I'll bring down on your family's head will have them wishing I *was* a blizzard or a drought."

"I'd like to see you try!" Evelyn fiercely cried. She wanted to hurt this woman, hurt her as she had never hurt anyone or anything.

Athena did a strange thing. She smiled and sat back and arched one of her eyebrows. "Would you, indeed? Perhaps that can be arranged." To Largo she said, "Escort her to the closet and bolt it. If she acts up, bind and gag her. I have an important decision to make and I do not wish to be disturbed."

"As you wish, mistress."

Evelyn got in a parting shot. "Don't say I didn't warn you."

A frantic search of The Armistead confirmed the contents of the note; Evelyn was gone.

His insides churning with worry, Zach joined his wife and the others in the lobby and sank despondently onto the couch. "If that woman harms a hair on her head—" He didn't finish the statement. There was no need.

Marshal Owen removed his hat to scratch his balding pate. "I have men out scouring the town. But that Borke woman has disappeared off the face of the earth."

"How can she hope to get away with it?" Lou asked. "The note she left is evidence enough to hang her."

"Unless she had Largo write it to shift the blame." Major Bannister was sipping a cup of coffee. "Or maybe it's just that she doesn't care anymore. After going to extraordinary lengths to cover her tracks, for her to brazenly take the child like this is baffling."

Shakespeare was pacing like a caged bear. Now he shook his fist and declared, "By my troth, I know not what to think of it. But I do know I can't stand around doing nothing. We should be out searching."

"My deputies will do a thorough job, I assure

you," Marshal Owen said. "I also sent men to each of the stables in case she tries to flee."

"Maybe she already has," said Lou, voicing the unthinkable.

Zach's headache was growing worse, not better. "Did anyone think to check the river landings? A horse isn't the only way out of town."

"No boats have left since noon," Marshal Owen said, "and the next isn't due to depart until eight tomorrow morning. I'll be there in person to screen the passengers. If that's her brainstorm, she won't succeed."

"I can't just sit here," Zach echoed Shakespeare's sentiments, and was out the door before his brain caught up with his feet. Lou ran after him, struggling to match his long strides.

"Slow down, will you?"

"I can't. I'm too wrought up." Zach was bubbling inside like a volcano about to explode.

"We'll find her," Lou said.

"We better." Zach came to the end of the block and turned down a side street. He had no set destination in mind. He just wanted to walk. To think. To come to grips with his seething emotions. After all he had been through, after Lou's abduction and his arrest for killing her abductors and being thrown in the stockade and then the ordeal of his trial and the relief of finally having it over, this was the straw that threatened to make him snap.

"No one would hurt Evelyn. She is too young. Too sweet."

Zach slowed so she could match his pace. "Until I was about seven, I thought the world was a wonderful place to live in. I had this idea everyone would get along and do as my father read to us in the Bible and love one another."

"We all think silly things when we're children."

"I'm not done. You see, about four years later the truth sank in. I realized people don't care about love and brotherhood and things like that. They would rather be at each other's throats. They would rather hate and maim and kill."

"That's too harsh," Lou said. "You don't give the human race enough credit."

"Harsh, is it? When whites hate Indians and Indians hate whites for no other reason than the color of their skin? When the Shoshones hate the Sioux and the Sioux hate the Blackfeet and the Blackfeet are at war with everybody? When counting coup counts for more than friendship?" Zach stopped and gazed at the buildings without seeing them. "My whole life has been about hate. At the rendezvous I was teased and sneered at and smacked because I'm a breed. White and red alike have always looked down their noses at me."

"I never have and I never will."

A grin of gratitude tugged at the corners of Zach's mouth. "You are my candle in the darkness. Until I met you, I had about decided people were worthless."

"And now?"

"I still think the world is a swamp of festering

evil. But when I look at you and think of how much you love me and how good you are, my own hate is quelled for a while."

"Love you I definitely do," Lou said, "and I always will." She kissed his cheek. "Two hearts entwined, forever."

Zach resumed walking. "All right. Enough of that." He focused on his missing sister. "We can't count on the marshal to find Evelyn. So where do we start?"

"The stables and the landings are covered. Where else is there?"

"Didn't Major Bannister tell you she rented a house under a false name? And later burned it down? What if it wasn't the only one? What if she is lying low somewhere until things quiet down and she can sneak off?"

"Could be," Lou said, "but how do we go about finding her?"

Zach was thinking fast and furious. "The newspaper carries rooms for rent, doesn't it? Let's go to their office and look through their back issues."

Lou grinned and snapped her fingers. "A great idea! Bannister also told me she arrived here about a week after you were thrown in the stockade. That should narrow our search."

The *Kansas Sun* was published out of a small building on Fourth Street. Zach asked to speak to the editor but it was Clarence Potts who came to talk to them.

"As I live and breathe! It's the boost in our circulation himself! To what do we owe the honor?"

Zach had never liked the reporter much. From what he had seen, reporters were like buzzards, forever picking at carrion in the hope of uncovering a juicy morsel. "We need your help."

"This is a switch," Potts said.

"My sister has been kidnaped by Athena Borke."

For all of ten seconds Potts was in shock. Then his reporter's instincts kicked in and his face underwent a transformation. Surprise gave way to crafty calculation. "That cute little girl I met at the landing? By the sister of the men you killed? This will be the biggest story ever!" He caught himself and asked, "What kind of help do you need?"

Zach explained their idea.

"Please, Mr. Potts," Lou said. "I know I didn't treat you very well when you came knocking at my door all those times. But a child's life is at stake."

"Did I say I wouldn't lend a hand?" Potts rejoined. "All I want is to come along. And for you to grant me full rights to the story. Meaning you talk to me and only me. No other reporters at all. Are we agreed?"

"Agreed," Zach said. "But I have a condition of my own."

"Name it."

"If we find the house, you must wait outside until it's over." Zach did not want the reporter to witness Athena Borke's death. It would not be a pretty sight.

"I'll miss everything," Potts complained.

"I want my sister back alive," Zach said. "One mistake and I could lose her. I must go in alone.

Once she's safe, you are welcome to do whatever you like." Zach's white half thought of a white custom to seal their arrangement. He offered his right hand. "Do we have a deal?"

Clarence Potts grinned like a kid given all the candy his heart desired. "You bet your life we do!"

Chapter
Seventeen

The farmhouse was on a low rise not far from the Missouri River. About half the acreage had been cleared for planting crops. The rest was thick woodland. The man who built the house had been forced to give up farming and move into town when one of the trees fell the wrong way and crushed his legs.

A woman calling herself Florence Meeker now rented the place. According to the former farmer, she was "a real beauty with the blackest hair you ever did see." She did not have a husband or children but she did have a man who worked for her. "About the biggest man alive," was how the farmer described him.

A narrow footpath wound through the woods to the house. The sun had set more than an hour ago and the woods were dark and still except for the rustle of the wind and the hoot of an owl.

As silent as a Comanche, Zach stalked along the path with his wife's Hawken in his hands. She was behind him, armed with her pistols. Neither of them made a sound, but the same could not be said of Clarence Potts. The reporter had all the stealth of a steam engine. He clomped along, snapping twigs and brushing against the undergrowth. They might as well be carrying torches, Zach thought to himself. "Try to be more quiet," he whispered, "or you'll give us away."

"I'm doing my best," Potts protested too loudly. "Beats me how either of you can see where to go."

"Maybe you should wait here," Lou whispered.

"Not on your life, lady. We have a deal, remember? I held up my end and helped you find Borke. Now I expect you two to hold up yours. I'll wait outside the house but not way out here."

"We will keep our word, Mr. Potts."

"Then let's get on with it, shall we? I don't much like being out in the wilds at night."

Zach inwardly laughed at the notion that this was wilderness. They were less than a mile from town and other farms were on either side. He moved on until the house reared out of the darkness. No lights were lit; it appeared deserted.

"What if she's not there?" Louisa whispered in his ear.

"We keep looking," Zach said. He would never give up. Not ever.

"Maybe we should wait for Shakespeare and Blue Water Woman," Lou remarked.

At Zach's request, Potts had sent an errand boy to The Armistead to tell them about the farmhouse. Zach expected them to show up anytime, but he couldn't wait. "Who knows what Borke and her servant have done to Evelyn?" He stalked grimly on.

Weeds had overrun the small yard since the farmer left. A trampled path between the woods and the porch showed that someone had recently been there, and might still be.

Zach motioned for Lou and Potts to stay in the trees. She nodded her understanding but Potts did not look pleased. Crouching, Zach dashed to the porch. He was about to put his foot on the bottom step when he changed his mind. Steps had a tendency to creak. Instead, he moved to the rail and climbed up and over.

The windows were not only closed, they were shuttered. An encouraging sign, Zach thought. Only someone who had something to hide would close up the house tight as a keg on such a hot, humid night. He padded to the door and reached out to try the latch, but a sound from inside froze him in place.

Backing off, Zach reconsidered. The door was bound to be locked. Kicking it in would warn Borke and Largo. There had to be a smarter way.

The farmhouse was two stories high. Only the bottom windows were shuttered.

Those on the second floor had drawn curtains. To reach them, all Zach had to do was climb onto the rail, shimmy up a post, hook a leg onto the overhang, pull himself up, then crawl to the nearest window and carefully pry at the sill. It opened with a slight scrape. Another moment, and he was hunkered in a bedroom.

A musty odor hung in the air. A bed was against one wall, a dresser against the other. The door was wide open.

A hallway brought Zach to a flight of stairs. A tingle ran through him when he saw a woman who must be Athena Borke bathed in the glow of a lamp. She was in a rocking chair, a straw hat on her knee, staring into an unlit fireplace. Crouching, he nearly shot her dead then and there. But just then a door across the room opened and in came Largo, limping slightly.

"Your tea will be ready in a few minutes, mistress."

"Thank you," Athena said.

Largo turned to go, but at the door he stopped and stared at her until she noticed.

"There is something else on your mind?"

"The girl, mistress. Murdering a child does not sit well with me. You know I would do anything for you, anything at all, but—"

Evelyn was alive, Zach realized. In his excitement he wanted to whoop for joy.

"Be at ease, Largo. I haven't made up my mind yet. Both choices appeal to me." Athena held out a hand and Largo came to her and gently clasped it in his. She dropped the straw hat to the floor and slowly stood. Their arms went around each other, their lips met in passionate release, and after a while Largo stepped back and bowed his head.

"Forgive my doubts. I am, as always, your obedient servant."

"And much more," Athena said. She tenderly stroked his square jaw. "I am sorry to put you through all this. My brothers were stupid but they *were* my brothers and their souls scream for vengeance."

"I have never complained, mistress."

"No. You never do."

Largo left, and Athena sat in the rocking chair with her chin in her hands, thinking. Her hair had fallen down over her shoulders and glimmered like a raven's feathers.

Slowly unfolding, Zach started down the stairs. He placed each foot where the steps met the wall instead of in the center. Once at the bottom, he stalked up behind the rocking chair and touched the Hawken's barrel to the nape of the woman's neck. "Not a peep or I will blow your brains out, bitch."

Athena Borke didn't cringe or cry out. She did not seem at all surprised or scared. Calmly turning her head, she said, "I should have known. But you won't kill me, breed. Not until you know your sister is safe."

"Where is she?" Zach was keeping an eye on the door Largo had gone through.

"Hand over your rifle and I'll tell you."

"Not a chance." Zach stepped to the right so he had a clear shot at her and the doorway, both. "You'll tell me anyway once I carve on you."

"My, my. You *are* vicious, aren't you?" Athena

mocked him. "How many people have you slain in your short span on this earth? Twenty? Thirty?"

"I never kill except in self-defense," Zach said.

"Liar. The war party you led against my brother's trading post wasn't done in self-defense. And you murdered my other brother in a tent in the dead of night. I read the army transcripts. I know all the details."

The woman knew nothing, but Zach was not going to stand there and justify himself.

"Think what you want. But I want my sister and I want her now."

"I have a better idea," Athena said. "Hand me that rifle and I won't have Largo shoot you in the back."

"Nice try," Zach said. He hadn't taken his eyes off the door once.

"There's another door behind you. He has a cocked pistol pointed at your spine. All I need do is nod and you're dead." Athena looked past Zach. "Isn't that right, Largo?"

"That is right, mistress."

Zach glanced over his shoulder. He had never heard the other door open, never heard the manservant enter. He could spin and fire but Largo would get off a shot and at that range couldn't miss. Since he couldn't rescue Evelyn if he were dead, Zach reversed his hold on the Hawken and handed it to the woman he hated with every fiber of his being.

"Who says breeds can't be reasonable?" Athena rose and trained it on him while stepping back. "Sit," she directed.

Zach hoped Lou had become tired of waiting and followed him in, as she had done at the tavern. "Where's my sister, damn you?"

"In good time," Athena answered. To her servant she said, "I saw a coil of rope in the shed out back when we were given a tour of the property. Fetch it, if you please."

Largo balked. "And leave you alone with him?"

"So long as we have Evelyn he won't dare resist." Athena sighted down the barrel. "And if he does—how did he phrase it? Ah, yes." She winked at Zach. "I will blow your brains out, you son of a bitch."

Lou shifted her weight from her right foot to her left and back again. It was taking Zach much too long, she decided.

Clarence Potts was fidgeting, too. "How much longer must we wait? He's taking forever."

"Another five minutes," Lou said. Then she was going in. Alone. The reporter would make too much noise and slow her down.

"To hell with that." Potts stood and marched past her. "This is the story of the year and I'm not letting it slip through my fingers."

"Wait!" Lou whispered, and grabbed at his pant leg, but he jerked loose. Moving from concealment, she snatched at his sleeve but he shrugged from her grasp.

"Don't try to stop me, Mrs. King."

"What if the woman and her servant are in there

and hear you?" Lou angrily demanded. "You're putting Zach's and Evelyn's lives in danger."

"I'm not as dumb as you seem to think," Potts arrogantly responded. "I'll sneak around back and go in that way."

His idea of "sneaking" left a lot to be desired; he simply tramped around the side to the back door. A shack and an outhouse were nearby but he didn't give them a second glance.

"See how easy that was?" Potts moved to the door and opened it and a gigantic hand wrapped itself around his throat. He squawked in fear as Largo emerged and with ridiculous ease lifted him off the ground.

Lou pointed both pistols but the reporter was in the way. As she sidestepped to the left to take aim there was a loud *crack*, and Largo hurled Potts at her. She had no time to duck or dodge. Bowled over, she winced as Pott's knee rammed into her stomach. She quickly shoved him and off and rose.

"No, you don't."

Lou found herself staring into the barrel of Largo's pistol. She might be fast enough to push it aside before he fired, but then again, she might not.

"Drop your weapons."

Lou dropped them.

"My mistress will be most pleased," Largo commented, and stooping, picked up a coil of rope he had dropped. He nudged Potts with a boot. His throat had been crushed and blood was coursing from his nose and mouth. "A reporter, if I'm not mistaken. I saw him at the trial. Why did you bring him along?"

"He wanted an exclusive," Lou said.

"Maybe they will grant him one in hell." Largo wagged the rope at the back door. "After you."

A teapot was on the stove, hissing and spitting. As they passed a closet Lou thought she heard a soft thump. The living room was cast in a rosy glow but there was nothing rosy about Athena Borke holding a rifle on Zach.

"What's this? I send you for rope and you bring me his slut? You have outdone yourself, Largo."

"You flatter me, mistress." The manservant lapped up the praise like a kitten lapping up milk. "There was a reporter with her. I disposed of him."

"Excellent."

Lou stopped beside the rocking chair. "I'm sorry. I couldn't stop Potts. He wouldn't listen."

"We've both blundered," Zach said, and squeezed her hand.

Athena Borke chortled at their display of affection. "Did you see, Largo? How touching. And how fitting. Bring the two chairs from the kitchen, would you, and place them back-to-back in the middle of the room."

The moment the giant left, Lou saw Zach tense to spring at Athena. But Athena noticed, too, and pointed the Hawken at her. "Go ahead, breed. Try, if you think you can reach me before a slug rips through your wife's belly."

Largo worked swiftly. He aligned the chairs back-to-back, and after Athena made Lou and

Zach take seats, he bound them by their ankles and wrists, then looped more rope around their waists.

The whole while, Lou's feeling of helplessness mounted. "What do you plan to do with us?"

Athena had lowered the Hawken and was smirking in triumph. "First things first. I believe good-byes are in order." She chuckled. "Largo, bring the girl."

"Yes, mistress."

Evelyn took one look and ran to Zach and flung her arms around his neck. Tears gushed and she clung to him, saying over and over, "Brother, brother, brother."

Lou couldn't see her husband's face but she felt his chair shake from the intensity of his emotions. The torment he was experiencing tore at her own heart. She saw Athena whisper to Largo, and suddenly the hulking manservant had Evelyn in one huge arm and was holding her off the floor.

"Let go!" Evelyn screamed, fighting furiously. But her punches and kicks had no more effect than those of a fawn in the grip of a grizzly.

"Harm her and I'll kill you!" Lou heard Zach vow. "So help me!"

Athena Borke walked up to Evelyn and tapped her cheek with a forefinger, and Evelyn tried to bite it but missed. "Hurt this wonderful child? Why, I wouldn't think of it. She has such a keen, inquisitive mind. I would much rather expand her horizons."

Lou responded when Zach did not. "How do you mean?"

Athena patted Evelyn's head. "She and I had the most marvelous talk. She's a fount of curiosity about the world and the people in it. It would be remiss of me not to show her."

"You wouldn't," Lou said.

"On the contrary." Athena poked Zach with a red fingernail. "Can you imagine how it will torture your husband? Knowing his sister is forever beyond his reach but always within my power? Why, I get goose bumps just thinking about how miserable he will be."

"Then you're not going to kill us?" Lou said. In which case they would trail her to the ends of the earth.

"Not him, no. But you on the other hand—" Shrugging, Athena stepped back, leveled the Hawken, and fired.

Chapter Eighteen

Shakespeare McNair had his life in the mountains to thank for his trim physique. Where most men his age had muscles gone to flab and guts of pure fat, Shakespeare looked twenty years younger and had the vitality and stamina of men half as old. It served him well as he jogged through the night on the heels of the errand boy sent by Clarence Potts. Beside him was Blue Water Woman.

"My kingdom for a horse," Shakespeare puffed. "Why didn't you tell us how far it was, boy?"

"Mr. Potts said to bring you on foot," the stripling responded, "and that's what I'm doing."

"Reporters," Shakespeare muttered. "They have marvelous foul linen."

Blue Water Woman glanced back, as she had done several times since leaving the hotel, but did not say why.

"Mr. Potts didn't want you there too soon," the boy said. "Something about spoiling his story."

"I'd like to spoil his face with a club," Shakespeare retorted. They had been winding along a dirt road marked by the ruts of wagon wheels but suddenly the boy veered into a patch of woods and along a footpath, but much more slowly.

"The house should be just ahead."

"It better be." Shakespeare was worried to his core about Evelyn, Zach and Lou. He loved all three as if they were the fruit of his own loins, and it would be more than he could bear if any were to die.

"Someone is following us, husband," Blue Water Woman announced.

Shakespeare looked. Dimly silhouetted against the night were two sprinting figures. "Get under cover," he commanded, and darted behind a maple. The pair never suspected the ambush until he leaped out at them. Recognition flooded through him, and he growled, "Bannister! Marshal Owen! What the blazes are you doing here?"

The major had drawn a pepperbox. "Are you trying to get yourself shot? You should know better."

Owen was doubled over, sucking in breath. "You didn't want us to follow you, McNair, but dammit, I'm a lawman. It's my job to arrest lawbreakers."

The boy came out of hiding. "Mr. Potts won't like this."

Shakespeare gave him a shove. "The man is tainted in 's wits. Let me worry about him and you worry about me."

"But Mr. Potts said only you and your wife. He was quite specific."

Shakespeare drew his tomahawk and held it so the edge was an inch from the boy's wide eyes. "And how specific would you say this is? Answer, thou dead elm, answer."

"He wants you to keep going," Blue Water Woman translated.

The house was only a short distance ahead. "There," the boy said, pointing. "Now my job is done." He bounded back the way they had come.

"What now?" Major Bannister asked.

As if in answer, a rifle boomed inside the house, and a high-pitched shriek keened like the wail of a stricken banshee. "That's Evelyn!" Shakespeare exclaimed, and bolted from the woods like a thoroughbred out of a starting gate. Blue Water Woman hollered for him to go slow, but he would be damned if he would when those he loved were in deadly peril. He charged onto the porch and rammed into the door at a full sprint, his shoulder lowered to absorb the brunt.

Wood shattered and slivers flew, and Shakespeare was spilled to his knees. But only for a moment. From the next room came Zach's anguished shout of, "No! No! No!"

In the grip of icy dread, Shakespeare hurtled through the doorway and came to an abrupt stop. His chest felt like it was ripped asunder.

Zach was struggling mightily to free himself from ropes that bound him to a chair, while in a chair behind his, slumped over with a spreading red stain high on her left side, was Lou.

"They shot her!" Zach raged. "They up and shot her!"

Blue Water Woman rushed in, the others close on her heels. Instantly she was at Louisa's side, cutting her free. "Help me, husband."

Shakespeare galvanized his numb mind into action. He helped to gently lower Lou to the floor and felt for a pulse. It was there but oh-so-faint. "She's alive." For how long was another matter.

"I'll find something to bandage her with, then one of us must go for the doctor." Major Bannister dashed back into the kitchen.

Zach was practically beside himself. "Cut me loose, damn it! Hurry! They're getting away! And they have Evelyn!"

Shakespeare's tomahawk made short shrift of the ropes. But it was not swift enough to suit Zach, he grabbed it and slashed the last rope himself, glanced once at Lou, and flew toward the rear of the house, a mercurial avenger who would not be denied.

"Go with him, husband," Blue Water Woman said. "We will tend to Lou."

Shakespeare did not need to be told twice. He emerged into the backyard just as Zach disappeared into the trees. "Wait for me!" he bawled, knowing full well Zach wouldn't. He was halfway across the yard when Marshal Owen came from the house and yelled the exact same thing to him.

Shakespeare ran as he had not run in ages. Branches tore at him and weeds tried to ensnarl his legs. He spotted Zach but could not keep him in sight. Not that he needed to. Fury had made Zach reckless and he was plowing through the brush like a bull gone amok, raising a hellacious racket in the process.

Shakespeare wondered where the woman and her servant were fleeing to. It wasn't town. Kansas was in the other direction. He hoped Zach was on the right scent and not plunging blindly along.

"McNair! Wait, damn it!" Marshal Owen bawled.

Shakespeare refused to stop. He might lose Zach entirely. A few more yards and the woods ended at a field. Mentally reaching deep down inside himself, he ran faster.

A grassy hill reared ahead. Zach was nearing the top. Shakespeare followed suit just as a shot shattered the night and Zach pitched into the waist-high grass. Veering, Shakespeare looped to the right to come up on the shooter from the side.

Marshal Owen drew a pistol, dropped to one knee, and fired at the small cloud of gunsmoke that marked the assassin's position.

Saving his own lead, Shakespeare tucked at the knees so only his head was above the grass and advanced until he spied a hunched form. He took aim, but the moment he did, the form flattened.

Patiently waiting for the shooter to show himself, Shakespeare glanced down the hill and saw that Marshal Owen had disappeared too, and must be making his way toward them. He had to be sure of his target or he might shoot the lawman by mistake.

A couple of minutes went by. Suddenly the grass behind Shakespeare crackled and a figure reared up. He instinctively brought his Hawken to bear but it was deflected by a forearm, and then Zach had hold of his shirt.

"Where's Largo?"

Shakespeare could care less about the manservant. "You're alive!" he said much louder than was prudent. "I thought you were done for."

"He missed, but not by much." Zach touched a razor-thin streak of blood on his temple. "Did you see where he got to?"

"Gone to ground," Shakespeare said, gesturing at the approximate spot.

"Like hell," Zach said. "Don't you see? He's delaying us. Giving Athena Borke time to get away with Evelyn." And with that, Zach was up and racing pell-mell down the other side of the hill.

"Don't!" Shakespeare cried, certain another shot would ring out. But none did. He started down the hill and was joined within a few strides by Marshal Owen.

"Here you are!" the lawman said. "Was that young King who went flying down there like a madman? He's lucky I didn't shoot him by mistake."

In the distance Shakespeare spied the shimmering surface of the Big Muddy. He also spied something else. Close to shore was a boat of some kind. "Is there a landing near this farm?"

Marshal Owen peered toward the Missouri River and shook his head. "No. Not that I know of."

Shakespeare thought no more of it until they had gone another fifty yards and the lawman made an observation.

"Say, my eyes aren't what they used to be, but I'd swear that boat is a paddle wheeler, by the bulge to stern. *Baby Josephine* was spotted upriver a day or so ago. Maybe it's her."

Although Shakespeare thought it best not to talk with Largo lurking somewhere close by, he could not help asking, "A steamboat?"

Owen nodded. "About a third as big as most. She's fast and easy to turn and can navigate in as shallow as five feet. Her captain hires out to anyone with the money to pay extra for the best."

"Dear God," Shakespeare said, and ran faster.

Trees sprinkled the terrain. A log nearly tripped them. Shakespeare was watching for more obstacles when Marshal Owen shouted a warning a heartbeat before a rifle cracked. Shakespeare ducked, but the shot hadn't been aimed at him. There was the sickening *splat* of the slug boring through flesh and the lawman clutched his chest and groaned and melted into the grass.

Throwing himself to the ground, Shakespeare tucked his Hawken to his shoulder. It puzzled him, Largo shooting at them and not at Zach. It defied logic, unless Zach were dead. Common sense told him to stay put, to let Largo make the next move. But there was the paddle-wheeler to consider, and the implications.

Rising, Shakespeare cat-footed toward a tree. He was a few steps from it when part of the trunk detached itself from the rest and a glittering blade sheared at his throat. He raised the Hawken in time to ward off the blow but the sheer brute force of the man swinging the knife knocked the rifle from his hands. He skipped backward and Largo came after him, a Bowie in each hand.

"Where is the breed, old man? It's him I want the most."

Shakespeare's response was to claw for his pistols. He swept one clear only to have it swatted from his grasp. The other was missing. Slipped out, Shakespeare figured, at some point in the chase. He drew his knife. "I don't know where he is."

Largo looked worried. "My mistress doesn't want him dead but I do. So long as he lives, he's a threat."

As if to prove him right, suddenly Zach was there, the tomahawk in his hand. He went for a death stroke but Largo countered and delivered a mighty stroke of his own. Steel sparked off steel. Thwarted, Largo flew at Zach like a Viking gone berserk.

Shakespeare had to do something. He sprang in

close and stabbed at Largo's ribs but Largo swatted his knife aside with almost casual indifference. Again Shakespeare leaped to help Zach. Again he failed to penetrate the manservant's guard.

Nothing was said. This was life or death. Shakespeare and Zach were skilled fighters but Largo was their equal. Their equal, and then some. For it soon became apparent that Largo Gandovar was the best knife fighter Shakespeare had ever encountered in a long life marked by countless run-ins with men supremely skilled at inflicting harm.

Zach was growing frustrated. His swings were more frantic, his slashes not nearly as precise.

Shakespeare knew why. Every moment Largo kept them there, every moment they were delayed, bought Athena Borke that much more time. He stabbed low and was blocked, stabbed high and didn't connect, then had to avoid having his head separated from his shoulders.

Suddenly Zach sprang back beyond Largo's reach and lowered the tomahawk. "This has gone on long enough."

Largo lowered his arms but only to his waist. "Not nearly, breed. My mistress can leave without me if she wants but this isn't over until you're dead."

"One of us will be, that's for sure," Zach said. Almost too swiftly for the eye to follow, his right arm flashed.

To Largo's credit, he tried to raise his Bowies but they were only as high as his chest when the tomahawk cleaved the bridge of his nose and buried itself between his eyes. Blood gushed, and Largo took a faltering step and feebly struck at empty air.

Zach was in motion before the giant body thudded to the ground. "Come on or we'll be too late!"

For months afterward Shakespeare had nightmares about their desperate race to the bank of the Missouri. He would see in his mind's eye the empty space where the paddle wheeler had been. He would hear the chug of a steam engine and be rooted in dismay as the boat vanished around a far bend. He would hear Zach's roar of rage, and add his own. And he would never be the same.

Five days later Deputy Morgan came to The Armistead. Lou was asleep in bed, a blanket pulled to her chin. It covered the bandages the doctor had applied that morning after he checked her stitches.

Zach was in a chair beside the bed. He hadn't slept much since the night at the farm and his eyes were bloodshot pits of sorrow.

Shakespeare and Blue Water Woman were by the window when the knock came, and Shakespeare went to answer it. "I hope you have good news."

Deputy Morgan shook his head. "I'm sorry, folks. I truly am. I sent riders downriver on the fastest horses in town and they caught up to *Baby Josephine* at Murphy's Landing, where she stopped to load lumber. They searched her from bow to stern but there was no trace of the Borke woman or Evelyn King."

"Did the captain know where they got to?" Shakespeare asked.

"That's just it," Deputy Morgan said. "Captain La Farge swears they were never on board. He says you were mistaken when you thought he put in to shore to pick them up."

"He has to be lying."

Blue Water Woman was deep in thought. "What if he was telling the truth? Athena Borke is clever. Maybe, while you were running to the river, she took Evelyn another way."

Shakespeare fought down tears. "Then they could be anywhere by now."

"It's next to hopeless," Deputy Morgan said.

"Like hell." Zach had risen, his eyes burning like fire. "Now that Lou is out of danger, I'm going after my sister. And heaven help Athena Borke."

WILDERNESS

Fang & Claw
David Thompson

To survive in the untamed wilderness a man needs all the friends he can get. No one can battle the continual dangers on his own. Even a fearless frontiersman like Nate King needs help now and then and he's always ready to give it when it's needed. So when an elderly Shoshone warrior comes to Nate asking for help, Nate agrees to lend a hand. The old warrior knows he doesn't have long to live and he wants to die in the remote canyon where his true love was killed many years before, slain by a giant bear straight out of Shoshone myth. No Shoshone will dare accompany the old warrior, so he and Nate will brave the dreaded canyon alone. And as Nate soon learns the hard way, some legends are far better left undisturbed.

___4862-0 $4.50 US/$6.50 CAN

LAURAN PAINE

GATHERING STORM

The two novels collected in this exciting volume capture perfectly the power and magic of Lauran Paine's work. His characters come alive, his plots create suspense, and his descriptions of the Old West are second to none. The title character in *The Calexico Kid* is a bandit who remains a mystery. Even those who have seen him cannot agree on what he looks like. How, then, can anyone bring him to justice? In *Gathering Storm,* two gunfighters arrive in a quiet range town within minutes of each other. One gunfighter in town is bad enough, but two can only mean trouble. Deadly trouble.

Dorchester Publishing Co., Inc.
P.O. Box 6640   ___5341-1
Wayne, PA 19087-8640 $4.99 US/$6.99 CAN

Please add $2.50 for shipping and handling for the first book and $.75 for each additional book. NY and PA residents, add appropriate sales tax. No cash, stamps, or CODs. Canadian orders require $2.00 for shipping and handling and must be paid in U.S. dollars. Prices and availability subject to change. **Payment must accompany all orders.**

Name: _____

Address: _____

City: _____ State: _____ Zip: _____

E-mail: _____

I have enclosed $_____ in payment for the checked book(s).

For more information on these books, check out our website at www.dorchesterpub.com.
_____ *Please send me a free catalog.*

GUNS IN
THE DESERT
LAURAN PAINE

This volume collects two exciting Lauran Paine Westerns in one book! In *The Silent Outcast*, Caleb Doorn is scouting for the U.S. Army when a small wagon train passes on its way to California. The train's path will take its members through Blackfoot country and the wagon master has foolishly taken a Blackfoot girl hostage. . . . In the title tale, Johnny Wilton, the youngest member of the Wilton gang, is shot and killed while attempting to set fire to the town. The surviving members of the gang plan a simple revenge—attack the town and kill everyone in it!
